S

MW01169064

Cozy Mystery Series Book Twelve

Hope Callaghan

hopecallaghan.com
Copyright © 2019
All rights reserved.

Visit my website for new releases and special offers: hopecallaghan.com

i

Acknowledgements

Thank you to these wonderful ladies who help make my books shine - Peggy H., Cindi G., Jean P., Wanda D., Barbara W. and Renate P. for taking the time to preview *Swiped in Savannah,* for the extra sets of eyes and for catching all of my mistakes.

Thank you to Alix, my Savannah expert, for sharing your knowledge of this special place.

A special THANKS to my reader review team:

Alice, Alta, Amary, Becky, Brinda, Carolyn, Cassie, Charlene, Christina, Debbie, Denota, Devan, Diann, Grace, Jan, Jo-Ann, Joyce, Jean K., Jean M., Judith, Katherine, Lynne, Megan, Melda, Kat, Linda, Lynne, Pat, Patsy, Paula, Rebecca, Rita, Theresa, Valerie, Vicki and Virginia.

Contents

Cast of Characters

Carlita Garlucci. The widow of a mafia "made" man, Carlita promised her husband on his death bed to get their sons out of the "family" business so she moves from New York to the historic city of Savannah, Georgia. But escaping the family isn't as easy as she hoped it would be and trouble follows Carlita to her new home.

Mercedes Garlucci. Carlita's daughter and the first to move to Savannah with her mother. An aspiring writer, Mercedes has a knack for finding mysteries, and adventure and dragging her mother along for the ride.

Vincent Garlucci, Jr. Carlita's oldest son and a younger version of his father, Vinnie is deeply entrenched in the family business and not at all interested in leaving New York for the Deep South.

Tony Garlucci. Carlita's middle son and the second to follow his mother to Savannah. Tony is protective of both his mother and his sister, which is a good thing since the female Garlucci's are always in some sort of a predicament.

Paulie Garlucci. Carlita's youngest son. Mayor of the small town of Clifton Falls, NY, Paulie never joined the "family business," content to live his life with his wife and young children away from a life of crime. His wife, Gina, rules the family household with an iron fist.

Chapter 1

Carlita Garlucci ran a clean rag over the top of the fireplace mantle and took a step back. "This place is spic and span and ready for our new tenant."

Mercedes, Carlita's daughter, joined her mother in the living room. "Yep, today is the big moving day. I hope Autumn likes her new apartment."

"I know Shelby and Violet, not to mention Tony, are all enjoying their new home." A look of concern crossed Carlita's face. "I hope we're not making a mistake in allowing Autumn to take Shelby's vacant unit."

Tony, Carlita's middle son, had recently married her tenant, Shelby. The newlyweds, along with Shelby's young daughter, had moved into a new, larger apartment above *Ravello's Italian Eatery*, Carlita's restaurant.

1

With the couple wed, she had two vacant units on her hands...Shelby's two-bedroom apartment, situated directly across the hall from Carlita and Mercedes' apartment, as well as Tony's efficiency, which was downstairs, and behind their pawnshop, *Savannah Swag*.

Autumn, who had recently broken up with her boyfriend, a local police officer, and whose lease was almost up in her current rental, was anxious to move out of the building where the couple both lived.

She nearly begged Carlita to allow her to rent the vacant unit. Despite her reservations about allowing a family friend to move in, Carlita had finally caved.

"Ma, we've been over this a dozen times. Autumn will be the perfect tenant and neighbor. Besides, she needs to get out of her building. It will be good for her to be closer to her brother, Steve."

"I suppose you're right. I just don't like to mix friends and business...it's never a good combination."

"It'll be fine. You'll see." Mercedes glanced at her watch. "I better get going. I promised Autumn I would help her move some of the smaller boxes this morning."

Carlita followed her daughter down the stairs and into the alley. "What on earth?" She frowned at the white minivan parked outside her door.

"Elvira has a company vehicle." Mercedes pointed to the bright blue lettering on the side of the van:

EC Security Services

EC Investigative Services

One Call Covers it All

Elvira's phone number and website information were listed directly beneath the catchy slogan.

"She's gonna have to move it." Carlita shifted her gaze. "We won't be able to get restaurant delivery trucks through here if she's hogging the only access to our unloading area."

"You better nip this in the bud before Elvira gets it in her head she owns the alley now that she bought the building behind us," Mercedes advised.

"I'm on it right now."

"See you later." Mercedes headed to their parking area. Carlita waited until she was gone before stepping around the back of the vehicle to her neighbor's rear entrance. She rapped loudly, but there was no answer. She returned to the vehicle and leaned inside the open driver's side window. "That figures." Fast food bags filled the passenger seat and spilled onto the floor.

A tower of coffee cup containers teetered precariously inside the cup holder, threatening to tumble. A strong stench - a combination of grease and sweaty feet - emanated from the vehicle.

Carlita made a gagging sound and jerked her head back. "Disgusting."

Certain that Elvira did not intend to move the vehicle without strong motivation, she strode down the sidewalk and to the business side of her neighbor's building.

A pair of newly installed black and white striped awnings shaded the entrance. Along with the awnings was a new sign, *EC Investigative Services*. Carlita spied movement inside and pushed the door open.

Beep. A loud buzzer announced her arrival. Dernice, Elvira's sister, hurried from the back. "Oh, it's you."

"I'm glad to see you, too."

"I thought you were a customer."

"Nope. Not a customer...just an aggravated neighbor."

"What did Elvira do this time?" Dernice grinned.

"Someone parked an *EC Investigative Services* van in the back alley. It's blocking delivery vehicles from reaching my restaurant."

"It's my fault. Sorry about that. I thought I was going to be in and out lickety-split," Dernice apologized.

Carlita's tone softened. "It's okay. I...it's just that we're sharing the alley. If the food trucks can't get back to my restaurant, there's nowhere else for them to unload."

"Right. I didn't think about that. You should've gone ahead and moved it out of the way."

"I would need the keys."

Dernice waved her hand. "I leave the keys in the ignition, that way I know exactly where to find them."

"Aren't you worried someone might drive off with the van?" Carlita remembered the trashed interior and foul odor. "Never mind. I don't think anyone would steal the vehicle smelling the way it does."

"That's Elvira's nasty natto. I told her the stuff stinks to high heaven but she claims she can't smell it."

"Speaking of Elvira...where is she?" Carlita glanced around, realizing she hadn't seen her nosy neighbor for a couple of days.

"She's managing the security gig over at *Darbylane Museum*."

"Ah." Carlita lifted a brow. "I heard there's some sort of famous exhibit in town. It's attracting a lot of attention and publicity."

"And with publicity comes crimes, so the city officials decided to hire the best security company in Savannah."

"*EC Security Services*," Carlita said.

"Yep. I'm on my way back there in a few. You should stop by and check out the exhibit. I'm not much into the artsy fartsy scene, but they have some cool old paintings."

"I might," Carlita said. "In the meantime..."

"Yeah. Move the van." Dernice followed Carlita out of the building, to the back and climbed behind the wheel.

"Gross." Dernice waved her hand in front of her face. "I was hoping if I rolled the windows down it would air out, but I think the smell is even worse now."

Dernice drove off while Carlita headed back inside. She stopped by the pawnshop to check on Tony and exited through the front entrance, turning right and making her way to *Ravello's*.

The recent grand opening of the Garlucci family's new restaurant had been a resounding success. Despite a few weeks of robust sales after opening, business had started to drop off, and it was slower than Carlita had anticipated. She knew she needed to get the word out so tourists and area residents would find out about her new restaurant.

She needed help, and she needed it fast. There was one person Carlita thought might be able to help - her friend, Glenda Fox, a member of the Savannah Architectural Society. Glenda, a longtime local, had plenty of connections not only in Savannah's Historic District, but also in the surrounding communities.

There were only a few diners inside *Ravello's* during the lunch hour rush. Carlita decided it was time to stop worrying and start working on drumming up business. She ran upstairs to grab her purse, and then hurried across the street to catch the next trolley to the *City Market* district.

She made it to the stop and only had a short wait before Reese and the trolley turned the corner. Reese gave a small wave as the trolley rolled to a stop.

"Hey, Reese." Carlita climbed the steps and settled onto the bench seat directly behind her friend.

"Hey, Carlita. Where ya headed?"

"*City Market*. I'm gonna try to track down Glenda Fox, Savannah Architectural Society's president. I'm hoping she can give me some pointers on drumming up business at *Ravello's*." Carlita cast an anxious glance out the window. "Now that summer is almost over, and we're in our official end-of-the-summer slump, I need to figure out a way to get more customers through the front door."

"I've been meaning to call you." Reese closed the door, and the trolley chugged away from the curb. "I've been giving it some thought. What about coupons?"

"Coupons?"

"Yeah. I was thinking if you had some coupons printed up, I could pass them out to trolley passengers when they board."

"Really?" Carlita leaned forward. "That's a great idea. Could you? I mean, is it against the trolley company's policy to promote area businesses?"

"Nah." Reese waved dismissively. "I've done it before. Pirate Pete gives me some to hand out every once in a while."

"Hmm." Carlita warmed to the idea. "Yes. Coupons might work."

"I'll be happy to help out."

"Thanks, Reese. You're the best."

The trolley reached the next stop and a large group of passengers boarded.

"You're busy today."

"Yep. We will be for the next couple of days. It's because of the *Darbylane Museum's* new exhibit." Reese waited for the passengers to find a seat before pulling back onto the street. "It's a mess."

"These riders are all trying to get to the museum?"

"Some of 'em, I'm sure." The trolley rounded the corner and turned onto Bay Street, the main thoroughfare that ran parallel to Savannah River.

"Crud." Reese hit the brakes, and the trolley screeched to a halt.

Carlita's eyes grew wide. "What on earth?"

Chapter 2

"Welcome to *Cotswold Georgian Exhibit* country," Reese said grimly. "The downtown city streets have been solid gridlock since yesterday."

"Because of the exhibit at *Darbylane Museum*?"

"Yep." Reese shifted gears, gunning the engine as she veered into the other lane and careened onto a narrow alley. "I can't wait 'til this exhibit thingy ends. It's making my job of maneuvering around town and reaching my stops a nightmare."

"It's that big of an event?"

"Today is by far the worst. There's an important and famous guest arriving soon to tour the exhibit which means the cops and city officials have blocked off even more of the streets."

Carlita was curious. "Do you know who the special visitor is?"

13

"Nope. Even the boss man is tight-lipped about the honorary guest. My friend, Dixie, the one who works at the Greyhound terminal, said she heard it was a duke or duchess." Reese attempted her best British accent. "Royalty from across the pond."

"A member of the royal family?"

"That's what Dixie heard. I don't care if it's the queen herself, I'm not going anywhere near that mess...not if I can help it."

With a couple quick turns down more narrow alleys and a near miss with a low hanging tree branch, they arrived at the *Elmwood Square* stop.

"If you plan to hitch a ride home on my trolley, come back to this stop. I can't get down the other square, at least for the rest of the afternoon."

"Will do. Thanks for the lift." Carlita gave her friend a thumbs up before making her way down the steps.

It was a short walk from the bus stop to the *Savannah Architectural Society's* office. The office was empty except for a receptionist at the front desk, a young woman Carlita had never met. She approached the counter. "Hi. I was hoping Glenda Fox might be in."

"She's over at *Darbylane Museum* greeting Savannah's special guest."

"Her, too?" Carlita shifted her purse.

"Yeah." The woman scooched forward. "I heard an honest-to-goodness duke from England is coming to town today to view the *Cotswold Georgian Exhibit*."

"I guess I should've called first to make sure she would be in the office. Do you know when she'll be back?"

"No, but she's going to be there for a while. I'm sure if you head that way, you'll be able to track her down."

"I took the trolley over here, and the driver had to turn off onto a side alley. We couldn't even get near the place. It's a madhouse."

"Isn't it exciting?" The woman beamed. "I wish I wasn't stuck here working so I could meet royalty." A dreamy look filled her face. "I wonder if he's married."

Carlita almost replied he was probably a hundred years old but didn't want to burst the woman's dream bubble. She thanked her for the information and stepped out of the office.

It would be at least another hour before Reese and the trolley circled back around. She reluctantly made her way to the end of the block. It was either wait here or join the crowd.

It wasn't much of a choice. She turned left and made her way to Bay Street. Pedestrians crowded the sidewalk. She moved from side to side, dodging tourists and bicyclists. There was even a group of tourists on Segways.

She neared the museum and noticed several local news vans lining the street. The area directly in front of the museum was roped off. A crimson carpet runner ran from the top of the steps all the way down to the end of the sidewalk.

She caught a glimpse of Glenda, standing off to the side with several other SAS members. Glenda's husband, Mark, was there, too.

Carlita's eyes scanned the clusters of people gathered together and talking loudly. There was a sudden movement near the museum's entrance as a uniformed security guard escorted a woman down the steps. It was Elvira.

She eased past several bystanders until she was standing on the other side of the velvet rope and at the bottom of the steps. "Elvira."

Elvira motioned for the woman to step beyond the rope.

Carlita waited until the woman walked away before trying a second time to get her attention. "*Elvira.*"

Elvira caught Carlita's eyes and hurried over. "Hey."

"You look pretty snazzy in your uniform," Carlita teased. "I almost didn't recognize you."

"It's new." Elvira brushed imaginary lint from the lapel of her jacket. "I figure I oughta look my best since I'm meeting royalty."

"How on earth did you get this job?"

"It was easy-breezy," Elvira cleared her throat. "You gotta know how to schmooze the right people. *EC Security Services* beat out four other bids to get this highly coveted gig. In the end, I presented them with an offer they couldn't refuse. This place is more secure than Fort Knox."

"So you bribed the person in charge of hiring the security company to guard the exhibit."

"Let's just say I greased a few palms. I may have also had to fudge a few things along the way, but you didn't hear it from me."

"It looks like every resident who lives in the city of Savannah is on hand."

"The crowds'll die down soon," Elvira predicted. "They're all waiting for prince...err, duke or whatever to show up. Last I heard his plane hadn't even touched down."

"Someone should let these people know."

"Mayor Puckett made an announcement, but it hasn't fazed them. I guess they don't have anything better to do on a Wednesday morning." Elvira shot Carlita a curious glance. "What are you doing here? An art exhibit doesn't strike me as your cup of tea."

"I'm waiting for Reese and the trolley to return. What do you mean...this isn't my cup of tea?"

"I dunno." Elvira waved dismissively. "I figured something to do with food or gambling would be more your speed."

"My son works at a casino, and I own a restaurant. That doesn't mean I don't appreciate the arts," Carlita said.

A woman dressed in a uniform identical to Elvira's and a nametag, *Astrid Herve*, joined them. "Bonjour."

"Bonjour," Elvira replied.

"La carte," the woman replied.

Elvira rolled her eyes. "You said menu. You're gonna have to keep working on your French, Astrid."

"I thought I said the crowds." The young woman eyed the growing masses. "The natives are starting to get restless."

"Well, we can't let 'em in yet." Elvira grabbed Carlita's arm. "I'm taking my neighbor on a quick tour. You stay here and hold down the fort for me until we get back. Try not to order croissants while I'm gone."

"Oui."

Carlita picked up the pace as Elvira propelled her along the sidewalk to the back of the building.

"Astrid is new. Business must be good. You're hiring more employees."

"Astrid was living on the streets. I found her digging through a dumpster and offered her a job. It's strictly under the table work so she could pick up some quick cash."

"No kidding. I think that's the kindest thing you've ever done."

"Eh," Elvira shrugged. "Just don't go telling anyone because you'll force me to have to deny it."

"You don't want people to think you're capable of being nice?"

"No. It will ruin my reputation. Anyhoo, it's only temporary until she can save up enough cash to buy a plane ticket out of here."

"She wants to move to France," Carlita guessed.

"Yep. Astrid is an old soul in a young body, a modern day hippie." Elvira stopped when they reached the rear entrance. "She reminds me of myself in my younger years."

The women climbed a narrow set of steps before entering a long hallway. Their shoes echoed loudly on the gleaming marble floor as they hurried to the other end.

"Where are we going?" Carlita whispered.

"To see the *Cotswold Georgian Exhibit*. I can't make heads or tails of some of the pieces." Elvira abruptly stopped in front of a marble column. "The exhibit pieces are in here."

As they stepped through the arched doorway, a rush of cool air blasted them, and Carlita shivered. "It's like the inside of a freezer in here."

"The exhibit floors are temperature controlled. Good for the art. Bad for the warm-blooded visitors. I'll show you the piece de resistance." Elvira stepped over to the wall and pointed to a small painting. "That's it...the one that looks like something threw up in a rainbow of colors."

Carlita stepped closer to the Plexiglas display case, her eyes narrowing as she studied the splashes of color. *A Piece of Renaissance.* She repeated the name. "It's...interesting."

"The museum's curator told me this painting is worth a small fortune." Elvira chuckled. "My artwork is ten times better than this. In fact, I could probably slip this baby under my jacket, stick one of my own paintings in its place and no one would be the wiser."

"I wouldn't try that."

"I wasn't serious. Of course, I wouldn't be dumb enough to take this ugly painting."

Carlita took a step back. "I must agree it appears to be a bunch of colors flung onto a canvas."

"You can have a quick look around if you want." Elvira followed Carlita around the room.

They stopped briefly to admire another piece of artwork before returning to the doorway.

"Thank you for the tour," Carlita said.

"You're welcome. Now for the best part." Elvira motioned Carlita to follow her. The women retraced their steps, returning to the back of the museum.

"In here." Elvira eased a swinging door open. The women stepped into a butler's pantry. An array of silver platters covered the counter.

Beyond the pantry, Carlita could hear the loud clanging of pots and pans, and she spied several kitchen workers darting back and forth.

"They got some good grub in the works." Elvira lifted the lid of one of the silver serving trays and plucked out a pastry. "These puffed pastries are delish. If these VIPs don't hurry up, all of these treats are gonna go to waste. Here have one." Elvira attempted to hand Carlita a tart.

"No thanks."

"Suit yourself." Elvira popped a lemon tart in her mouth before grabbing two more. She carefully wrapped them in a cocktail napkin and shoved them in the front pocket of her jacket. "We better get back to the festivities. His lordship or whatever he is should be here soon."

The women stepped out of the building and returned to the front of the museum. Astrid was standing in the same spot. "It looks like the guest of honor has finally arrived."

"I'll let you get back to work." Carlita thanked Elvira for the tour and skirted the edge of the large crowd, searching for her friend, Glenda.

She finally gave up and crossed to the other side of the street before backtracking to Reese's trolley stop where a long line of passengers stood waiting.

Reese and her trolley arrived right on time. Carlita let the others board before following them up the steps. A *reserved* sign blocked her usual spot.

"This trolley is almost full." Carlita peered anxiously down the aisle in an attempt to locate an empty seat.

"That's why I saved your spot." Reese plucked the sign from the seat.

"You saved the seat for me?"

"Of course. Gotta save the best seat in the house for one of my best buds."

"Reese, you're a doll." Carlita plopped down. The arches of her feet ached, and she wiggled her toes. "What a zoo."

"Told ya." Reese pulled the door shut and consulted her rearview mirror before steering the trolley onto the street. "I bet the museum is a madhouse...wall-to-wall people."

"I just left there. You were right - the city officials were waiting on a guest of honor, a duke or some such thing. Elvira and her gang were on hand."

"Better you than me," Reese quipped. "Elvira's security company is managing the event?"

"Yes."

"Business must be booming. I see her people all over town these days."

"She's building a name for herself. Whether she's above board in getting the business is another story." Carlita thought about Elvira's company van blocking the alley. "She purchased a new van."

"That's the best news I've heard all day. Now I won't have to worry about her trying to weasel free rides from me." Reese and Elvira had been at odds ever since the time Elvira attempted to interrogate a couple of Reese's riders.

Reese warned her to knock it off; Elvira became angry and filed a complaint against her. "Good riddance."

The conversation shifted to talk about the area's upcoming festivals. "Maybe I should start looking into joining some of the food festivals to get *Ravello's* name out there."

"I hadn't thought of that. Yes. You might be onto something," Reese said. "Have you had any luck renting out your vacant apartments?"

"We rented the two-bedroom across the hall from me to Autumn Winter, a family friend. In fact, she's moving in today."

"One down, one to go. I better get to work." Reese reached for the microphone and began narrating their trip, pointing out various points of interest to the trolley riders.

They reached Carlita's stop. She gathered her things before carefully navigating the narrow steps. "Thanks for saving me a seat."

"You're welcome. Good luck with your new tenant."

"Thanks. I'll see you later." Carlita gave her friend a quick wave before hurrying across the street and into the pawnshop.

The bell chimed, and Tony, Carlita's middle son, gave her a quick look. She made her way across the store and waited for him to finish helping a customer. "I was lookin' for you earlier. Shelby wanted me to give you the rest of the keys to her apartment."

"I already changed the locks." Carlita followed her son to the back of the store. He reached inside the desk drawer and pulled out a set of keys before handing them to his mother. "I asked Josh to give Autumn a hand with moving some of her larger pieces of furniture up the stairs."

"That's nice. I'm sure she appreciates it. Isn't Autumn's brother, Steve, here to help?"

"He couldn't make it over until later. Sam was home. He heard the commotion in the hall, came out to see what was going on and he's helping, too."

"I'm sure Mercedes is thrilled," Carlita joked.

"She might not be thrilled, but Autumn doesn't seem to mind."

Carlita lifted a brow. "Autumn told me she was swearing off men for a while."

"It's lookin' like she may have already changed her mind," Tony said. "Have you made a decision on my old efficiency?"

"Yes." Carlita was having difficulty finding a long-term tenant for Tony's former unit. Although the efficiency was ready to move into, it was only large enough for one, possibly two people. The few prospective tenants she'd shown it to had turned up their noses when they found out how "cozy" it was.

The last person to view the unit told Carlita it reminded her of an extended-stay hotel room. When she told Mercedes what the woman had said, her daughter suggested they consider leaving Tony's furniture in the unit and turning it into a short-term rental.

"We're going to turn it into a short-term rental." Carlita had done her homework and discovered they could double their income if they rented the efficiency short-term. Mercedes agreed it was a wise move and began running ads for weekly and monthly rentals.

Several promising prospects had submitted applications online. Mercedes had offered to start scheduling appointments to meet with the prospective tenants.

Carlita thanked her son for the extra set of keys. She made her way into the narrow hall, squeezing past a television stand before climbing the stairs to the second story landing.

The door to Autumn's apartment was wide open. Carlita heard a loud thump followed by a cuss word.

"Is everything okay?" She cautiously approached the doorway and peeked around the corner. Josh and Sam were moving a sofa around the living room.

Autumn stood off to the side. "Shift a little to the right and...you've got it."

"Is this thing filled with lead?" Sam joked.

"No. It's a sleeper sofa."

"Might as well be filled with lead," Josh grunted.

Autumn caught Carlita's eye. "Hi, Mrs. G."

"Hello, Autumn. I thought I would stop by to see how you're doing. It looks as if Sam and Josh have it under control."

Mercedes carried a box into the apartment and set it on the floor. "Hey, Ma. Autumn has almost finished moving in."

"Where are your movers, Autumn?"

"More like losers," Autumn joked. "I hired a couple of part-timers from the newspaper to help me move the heavy stuff. When they got here and saw the stairs, they skedaddled. Thankfully, Tony came out to see if I needed any help. He asked Josh to give me a hand. Sam stopped by to check on us and graciously offered more muscle."

Sam straightened his back. "Those are some steep stairs."

"It looks like we're done moving the big stuff," Josh said.

"Yes, and thank you so much," Autumn said. "I don't know what I would've done."

"You're welcome. I better get back to work." Josh slipped out of the apartment, his heavy steps thumping loudly on the stairs. The back door to the pawnshop slammed shut.

Carlita turned to Sam. "Thank you for saving the day."

"I couldn't leave a lovely damsel in distress," Sam teased.

Autumn clasped her hands, and Carlita could've sworn the young woman nearly swooned. "Saying thank you doesn't seem like enough. As soon as I get settled, I'm going to invite you over for dinner."

"You don't have to."

"Uh." Autumn shook her head. "I insist."

"What about me?" Mercedes frowned. "What am I? Chopped liver?"

"I'll invite you over one of these days, too." Autumn smiled widely, never taking her eyes off Sam.

"You're welcome." Sam strode to the door. "I better get going. I have a large tour group booked for this afternoon. We're making a special stop at *Darbylane Museum*."

"It's a madhouse over there," Carlita warned. "I stopped by while I was waiting for Reese and the trolley. There's a guest of honor, some sort of duke or something. The place is packed."

"By the time I get there, the crowds will have cleared." Sam stepped into the hallway and Autumn hurried after him. "About dinner...how does Friday night sound?"

"I'll have to check my calendar." Sam smiled. "Good luck with the rest of the move."

Carlita waited until he was gone. "That was very nice of Sam...and Josh to help you move."

"Right." Mercedes made a small snorting sound. "I need to take care of some things myself. See you later, Autumn."

"Thanks, Mercedes."

"This is for you." Carlita handed her new tenant the mailbox key. It's the mailbox key."

Carlita explained she had a master key, to all of the units. "I'll only use it in the event of an emergency." She nodded in the direction of Sam's unit. "You and Sam seemed to hit it off."

"We knew each other from before. Sam and my ex are friends," Autumn explained. "I don't think Mercedes was too keen on having him help, but there was no way Josh and the two of us could've carried my sofa up the stairs."

"Don't worry about Mercedes." Carlita patted her arm. "She and Sam don't see eye to eye. If you need anything else, you know where to find us."

Autumn trailed behind Carlita and followed her into the hall. "Thanks again for letting me move in, Mrs. G. You won't be sorry."

"You're welcome." Carlita smiled softly. "I have a feeling you're going to spice things up around here."

Little did Carlita know how exciting things were about to become.

Chapter 3

Carlita returned to her apartment and found her daughter sprawled out on the sofa, television remote in hand and a sour expression on her face.

She set her purse on the table next to the door. "You look cranky."

"Sam Ivey makes me cranky." Her daughter turned the television off and tossed the remote on the coffee table. "I regret the day that man moved into our building."

"Even more than the day Elvira moved in?" Carlita teased.

"Yes...maybe. I don't know. It's a tie."

"I don't understand why you dislike Sam so much." Carlita eased onto the edge of the recliner and eyed her daughter. "He's always so helpful. Look at what he did for Autumn today."

"He offered to help because he wanted to get under my skin."

"Mercedes," Carlita chided. "Are you telling me you think Sam offered to help Autumn move her furniture because he thought it might irritate you?"

"He *knew* it would irritate me. And then he had the nerve to invite himself to dinner at Autumn's place."

"You're wrong. I was there. Autumn was the one who invited Sam to dinner, to thank him for helping."

"But he was fishing for an invitation." Mercedes sprang from the sofa. "I think I need some fresh air. I'm going to check out the art exhibit that's all over the news."

"It's wall-to-wall people down there."

"You already went and didn't ask me to go along?"

"No." Carlita explained she tried to track down Glenda Fox. "I had time to kill before Reese and the trolley circled back around, so I decided to see it for myself. Elvira and her company are handling the security for the event."

"Maybe she'll let me in for free." Mercedes headed to her room and returned with her backpack. "I'm gonna take my Segway instead of the trolley. It'll be faster."

"Don't say I didn't warn you."

Mercedes promised her mother she would return before dark and slipped out of the apartment. Since Carlita was the greeter at the restaurant that evening, she grabbed a bite to eat and headed out.

The next couple of hours passed quickly despite several lulls in the crowd, which concerned Carlita. After closing for the evening, she helped the wait staff tidy the dining room.

The chef was the last to leave. Carlita locked up and limped down the alley to her apartment.

Mercedes and her Segway careened around the corner. She waited on the stoop while her daughter hopped off. "Did you enjoy the art exhibit?"

"No." Mercedes unclipped her helmet. "I changed my mind. I decided to stop by the *Thirsty Crow* to say 'hi' to Cool Bones and his band instead. The place was packed."

"I need to get down there one of these days." Carlita thought of the light dinner crowd at *Ravello's*. "At least someone is busy."

She held the door and waited for her daughter to steer the Segway inside. "Tony stopped by the restaurant earlier. I forgot to ask him about Shelby's follow-up doctor visit. It was either today or tomorrow."

Before Tony and Shelby's recent wedding, her new daughter-in-law was exhibiting concerning symptoms of exhaustion and dizzy spells. Not long after returning from their brief honeymoon, Shelby visited her doctor who ran several tests on her.

"It's tomorrow. I'm covering at the pawnshop while Tony goes with her." Mercedes told her mother she was heading to her room to work on the book she was writing while Carlita carried the restaurant's receipts and cash box to her desk.

She made it through part of the paperwork, and then the lines on the computer screen began to blur. Carlita removed her reading glasses and rubbed her eyes, wondering for the umpteenth time if she hadn't taken on more than she could handle, between the apartment rentals, the pawnshop and now the restaurant.

She still needed to find a tenant for the vacant efficiency downstairs. Although Carlita had reservations about letting Autumn move in, she was relieved the unit was finally rented.

Carlita gave up trying to focus and trudged off to bed. Despite her exhaustion, she had trouble falling asleep, her mind bouncing from *Ravello's* to Shelby's health to Mercedes' aggravation with Sam.

Her daughter was interested in Sam, and Carlita was certain the feeling was mutual. Autumn had inadvertently inserted herself in the middle of their strained relationship.

She hoped it wouldn't affect the girls' friendship, and Carlita wondered if perhaps she should hint to Autumn there was more to Sam and her daughter's relationship than met the eye. She finally decided it was best not to stick her nose in where it didn't belong and to let the situation play out.

On the flip side, perhaps a little green-eyed monster was exactly what Mercedes needed to admit she had feelings for Sam after all.

*****

Rambo woke Carlita early the next morning, pawing at her bedroom door. She stumbled out of bed and slipped into her bathrobe. "Let's go."

Her pooch led the way down the steps and into the alley. Carlita noticed Elvira's kitchen lights were on, which was unusual since Elvira and her sister weren't typically morning people.

It was an easy walk to the end of the alley and Rambo's strip of grass near the edge of the parking lot. He took care of business before patrolling the perimeter of his small green space.

"Let's go before someone sees me standing out here in my pajamas." Carlita coaxed him back to the apartment. Wide-awake, she knew there was no way she could go back to sleep.

Instead, she started a pot of coffee and settled in at the computer. Carlita scanned her emails before finishing her banking and then took a quick look at the morning's headlines. Her breath caught in her throat when she read the caption:

"Priceless artwork stolen right out from under the nose of the security company hired to keep it and the Cotswold Georgian Exhibit safe."

The news story explained a valuable piece had been stolen the previous evening from *Darbylane*

Museum. The story hinted at the theft being an inside job.

Elvira's company, *EC Security Services*, was mentioned. The last sentence told that the authorities had detained at least one individual in connection with the stolen artwork.

Carlita shoved her chair back. It toppled over, crashing onto the hardwood floor. "Whoops." She righted it before stepping outside and onto the balcony. She stared at the back of Elvira's building.

Mercedes dashed out of her room. "What's going on? I heard a big crash."

"Sorry. I tipped my chair over. I was just looking at Elvira's apartment."

Mercedes traipsed across the living room and joined her mother. "What did Elvira do this time?"

"Someone swiped a priceless piece of art from *Darbylane Museum,* the one that Elvira and her company were hired to keep an eye on. The authorities have detained someone as part of the investigation. They claim it was an inside job."

"Elvira?" Mercedes' jaw dropped.

"I don't know." Carlita pointed to the dim light in the window of the building across the alley. "Elvira's lights are on. She's normally not a morning person."

"I guess we'll find out soon enough." Mercedes covered her mouth to stifle a yawn. "Excuse me. This isn't my time of the day."

"I'm sorry I woke you."

"It's okay. I needed to get up and get ready. I promised Tony I would cover for him at the pawnshop while he and Shelby visit the doctor this morning for her follow-up visit."

Carlita followed her daughter into the kitchen. "Hopefully, Shelby's doctor will have a good report. I know he ran a bunch of tests on her to try to figure out what's going on."

"I hope so." Mercedes poured a cup of coffee and headed to the bathroom to get ready while Carlita returned to her desk.

Determined to get serious about renting out Tony's old efficiency unit, Carlita sorted through her emails and clicked on a short-term application submitted the previous day.

"Still reading the headlines?" Mercedes emerged from the bathroom, her hair wrapped in a towel.

"No. We have another short-term application. This one sounds intriguing."

Mercedes leaned over her mother's shoulder. "Angelica Reynolds. The name sounds familiar."

Carlita, still seated at the desk, scooched to the side to make room for her daughter.

"Oh my gosh! It's Angelica Reynolds."

"Who is Angelica Reynolds?"

"She's a famous mystery/thriller writer. I've read several of her books." Mercedes let out a high-pitched squeal. "She's coming here, to Savannah. I heard they're making a movie out of her book, *Into the Night*."

Mercedes reached for the mouse. "Ma. We have to let her move in. I can pick her brain. Maybe she'll pull some strings and get us on the set of the movie as extras."

"Oh no." Carlita began shaking her head. "No way am I going to be in a movie."

"I would do it. This is the chance of a lifetime. When does she want to move in?"

"Soon." Carlita squinted her eyes and studied the screen. "This weekend or early next week."

"Perfect." Mercedes clapped her hands. "I'll handle this. I'll give her a call to schedule a time for her to come by to check out the unit."

"Don't let the stars in your eyes keep you from making a sound judgment. She still has to pass muster. I want a good, solid tenant, a good neighbor and someone drama-free," Carlita warned.

"Don't worry. I'll make sure she's a model tenant. I think she'll be a perfect fit." Mercedes rushed back to the bathroom to finish getting ready, and then mother and daughter switched spots.

Carlita climbed into the shower and began washing her hair. She thought about the missing artwork at the museum. There were masses of people on hand for the exhibit. The authorities must believe they had a solid lead to have detained someone already.

What if Elvira had taken one of the paintings? She made a joke about it, not to mention she was quite comfortable navigating the museum and had no qualms about wandering around inside.

Carlita finished showering and began rummaging around in her closet. It was early fall, and while most of the days were sunny and warm, the mornings were cooler. She finished dressing and stepped into the small hall where she heard voices coming from the front of the apartment.

"Hello, Autumn." Carlita greeted her new tenant, who was standing in the dining room talking to Mercedes. "You're up early."

"I'm on my way to work," Autumn said. "I stopped by to find out if you're still looking for a tenant for the efficiency unit downstairs."

"Yes. We're still searching," Carlita said.

"No." Mercedes shook her head. "I think we found someone. Besides, Ma and I decided to turn it into a short-term rental unit."

"Really?"

"The famous author, Angelica Reynolds, is interested in it."

"I've never heard of her," Autumn said. "An author, huh?"

"You've never heard of Angelica Reynolds?" Mercedes gasped.

"Don't worry, Autumn. Neither have I."

"I wanted to thank you again, for letting me take the apartment. The timing was perfect for me to move in. Sam Ivey living in the same building is an added bonus."

Mercedes made a small grunting sound. "He can be a jerk."

Carlita ignored her daughter's comment. "Sam is a wonderful tenant, and so is Cool Bones. I'm sure you'll like living here."

"I already do." Autumn glanced at her watch. "I better get going before I'm late for work."

"And I better get downstairs to meet Tony and open the pawnshop." Mercedes dashed out the door and Autumn followed her.

Grayvie, Carlita's cat, began circling her feet. She reached down and patted his head. "I know. It's time for breakfast." She finished filling her pets' food dishes before pouring another cup of coffee and wandering out onto the deck with Rambo.

Her first task of the day was to meet with *Ravello's* chef to start tweaking the restaurant's menu. She planned to eliminate several of the items that weren't selling and try to find some new ones to spice things up, not to mention add additional profit to the restaurant's bottom line.

She returned to the computer where she found a new appetizer and an entrée, both of which sounded promising. She printed copies before shutting her computer off.

It was time to check on Mercedes to see if she needed help. Carlita unplugged her cell phone from the charger and noticed she'd missed a call.

It was her friend, Glenda Fox. The call was recent. Carlita checked her volume noticing she'd turned the ringer off.

She dialed her friend's number and the call went to voice mail. "Hey, Glenda. It's Carlita. I see I missed your call. I stopped by the SAS yesterday to pick your brain. I need some help drumming up business for *Ravello's*."

She asked her friend to return the call before slipping the phone into her pocket. "C'mon, Rambo. Let's check on Mercedes."

Carlita and her pooch exited the apartment at the same time Cool Bones, aka Charles Benson, stepped out of his.

"Hello, Carlita."

"Hi, Cool Bones." Carlita pointed to the saxophone case her tenant was holding. "You on your way to practice?"

"Yes, ma'am. Mercedes stopped by the *Thirsty Crow* last night to say 'hi.' I was telling her we got a big gig coming up over at the convention center." Cool Bones motioned to Autumn's unit. "I see you rented Shelby and Violet's old apartment to Autumn Winter."

"Yes. Now all I have to do is find a tenant for the efficiency downstairs. I think we're going to start doing short-term rentals."

"You don't say. I'll keep my ears open and let you know if I hear of anyone who might be interested."

"Thank you. I'll take all the help I can get."

Cool Bones joined her, and they made their way down the steps to the hall. "Looks like it's gonna be a beautiful day."

"Yes, it does. Have a good one." Carlita watched her tenant exit the building before opening the pawnshop's back door.

The store was busy for a Thursday morning. Carlita jumped in to help her daughter and the part-time employee.

Glenda returned Carlita's call, but she was busy helping a customer, so she let it go to voice mail. Finally, there was a quiet moment. She stepped out of the pawnshop before listening to her friend's message.

"Hi, Carlita. Glenda here. Sorry I missed your call. I'm sure you've heard about the art exhibit at *Darbylane Museum*. Elvira and her security company were hired for the event. You'll never guess what she did." Glenda ended the cliffhanger call, asking her friend to call her back.

Chapter 4

She quickly dialed the number.

"Hey, Carlita."

"Hi, Glenda. I got your message, something about the art exhibit and Elvira."

"Yeah. I'm right around the corner from your place. I figured I would swing by so we can talk in person."

"I'm standing in front of the pawnshop," Carlita said.

"I'll be there in less than a minute."

Carlita rounded the corner, nearly colliding with her friend. They both took a quick step back.

"You weren't kidding about being right around the corner," Carlita joked.

"It's such a nice morning; I figured I would walk over." Glenda slid her cell phone into her front pocket. "Elvira is down at the police station being questioned about *Darbylane Museum's* missing artwork."

Carlita remembered the conversation with Elvira, how she joked about swapping out one of the pieces of artwork for one of her own. "You wouldn't happen to know which piece is missing, would you."

"*A Piece of Renaissance.* It's rumored to be worth millions."

"Elvira gave me a private tour of the museum yesterday. She pointed out that particular piece, made a joke about how she could swap it out and no one would even notice."

"You don't think..." Glenda's voice trailed off. "No. Elvira has been known to do a lot of dumb things, but she would have to be off her rocker to steal that piece of art."

"All I can say is if she thought she was being funny and played a prank, it backfired."

"Unfortunately, our names are also getting thrown around. The authorities called me first thing this morning to ask me a few questions."

"Why you?"

"Because Elvira listed me...listed *us* as references."

"Us?" Carlita shook her head.

Glenda pointed to Carlita. "You and me. She used both of our names as references on her application to get the job at the museum."

"I...I never told her she could use me as a reference."

"And neither did I, but that didn't stop her from doing it, which is why the authorities wanted to talk to me. In fact, I'm sure you're on their list to contact, as well."

"Great." Carlita frowned. "That woman has caused me more trouble since she moved out of my building than during the time she lived under my roof."

"Including the time she set her apartment on fire?" Glenda joked.

"Let me revise my statement. She causes me as much grief now as when she lived under my roof. I hope she didn't take the painting, even if it was a prank. She'll never work in this town again."

"I agree." Glenda changed the subject. "How's business these days? Mark and I plan to stop by for dinner this Saturday evening."

"We have busy days and slow days. The first couple of weeks after we opened we were going gangbusters. Since then, business has started to taper off. I'm not sure if it's because of the change in seasons or if this is the new norm." All of Carlita's concerns over the success or failure of her business came flooding back. "That was the reason I stopped by to see you yesterday."

"You're looking for some advice?"

"Yes. I was also wondering how Mark's new venture, *Savannah Riverfront Inn*, is doing."

"We're in the same boat. Some days are great while others are crickets. Like any tourist town, there are ups and downs." Glenda eyed her friend thoughtfully. "You could try coupons or discount cards."

"Reese suggested something similar, how I should experiment with coupons. She offered to hand them out to trolley passengers."

"Why don't we join forces?" Glenda brightened. "We could give you discount cards for the inn, and you give us cards for the restaurant."

"What a great idea. Thanks, Glenda." Carlita motioned toward the apartment. "Would you like to come in for a cup of coffee?"

"No." Glenda consulted her watch. "I need to get back to the other side of town. I called an emergency meeting with the other members of the

SAS to see if they've heard anything about the theft."

Carlita thanked her for the heads up concerning Elvira. She promised to begin working on discount cards for the restaurant and then returned to the apartment to grab the recipes before circling around to the alley.

"Hey!" Elvira stood in her doorway.

"Hello, Elvira." Carlita crossed to the other side. "You look frazzled."

"I've had my hands full. Listen, I was wondering if it would be okay if I used you as a business reference."

Carlita briefly closed her eyes. "It's a little late for that, isn't it?"

"What do you mean?"

"You already used me as a reference. In fact, I'm waiting for the authorities to come knocking on my door to ask me about the missing piece of artwork you joked about taking yesterday."

"I-I...uh. I was kidding about that," Elvira stuttered. "You know I was just kidding. I even told you it was a joke."

"Yes, you did, but it doesn't mean you didn't say it."

"You're not going to tell anyone what I said, are you?"

"Only if they ask me," Carlita said. "I'm not going to lie. Did you take the painting?"

"No." Elvira's eyes grew wide, and she shook her head. "Do you think I'm stupid?"

"No. Stupid isn't your first trait that comes to mind. You have other more prominent characteristics, including a disregard for rules and laws. If you didn't take the artwork as a joke, what exactly did happen?"

"I was working my shift. The place was a madhouse, people coming and going, spilling food and drinks. It was a full-time job keeping the crowds from messing with the artwork." Elvira explained she strategically positioned her employees in and around the building and appointed herself as the one to keep an eye on *A Piece of Renaissance*. "I figured I should be the one to keep an eye on the art."

"When exactly did the piece in question go missing?"

"It happened after the museum closed. Dernice was in charge of checking every nook and cranny of the museum to make sure no one was hiding out, waiting for us to lock up. The museum curator accompanied me for a final inspection of the museum and grounds, we locked the doors and left."

"So why are you considered a suspect?"

"Because after we locked up, I told Spelling, the curator, I accidentally left my keys on the counter of the butler's pantry. I went back in to get them while he waited for me. I picked them up, joined him in the hallway and we left together. The last thing he did was set the alarm."

"Then I'm sure the authorities cleared your name," Carlita said.

"Logically, most intelligent life forms would reach the same conclusion, except that I was the last person inside the building before the alarm was set. When the curator and staff arrived first thing this morning, the piece was MIA."

"So maybe someone...a staff member took it," Carlita theorized.

"I said the same thing myself, but the cops aren't talking. I'm not taking the rap for the piece of garbage painting. I told them they could search this whole place, my van, whatever, but I wasn't going to go down for this. My reputation is at stake."

"I think..." A truck turned onto the alley and coasted by them, interrupting their conversation.

It was Carlita's chef, Dylan. "I gotta get going." She stepped off the stoop. Elvira trailed behind. "You're not going to mention me joking about the missing artwork, are you?"

"I already told you I'm not going to lie."

"But you can't tell them that. They're going to throw me in the slammer, for sure."

"Then you'll have to work harder to prove your innocence." Carlita stopped abruptly. "Listen, you said you have nothing to hide. I'm going to be honest and truthful. Besides, this is partly your fault." She began walking again.

"How so?" Elvira refused to give up, and she fell into step.

"For using me as a reference without my permission." They reached the back of the restaurant. "I wouldn't even be on the investigator's radar if you hadn't used me as a reference."

Elvira's shoulders slumped as she watched Carlita step inside the restaurant. "Maybe you'll get lucky, and they won't want to talk to me."

"Fat chance." Elvira trudged off, and Carlita shook her head as she sucked in a breath.

Dylan parked his vehicle and joined her. "Who was that?"

"Elvira Cobb, my former tenant, a royal pain in the rump, and a woman who is always managing to become involved in some sort of crisis." Carlita forced Elvira's dilemma from her mind as she handed Dylan a small stack of papers.

"I've found a few recipes we could try. I thought we could pick them out together, and then I'll do a test run in my kitchen."

Dylan and Carlita headed inside to a booth near the back. They mulled over the possible picks and decided on a new lunch special, along with a chicken Milano recipe.

Carlita studied the list of ingredients. "This should be fairly simple and something we can make in large quantities."

"What are the ingredients again?"

"Chicken breasts, fettuccine, heavy cream, fresh basil, sundried tomatoes."

"Sounds good."

The two of them went over the upcoming workweek schedule as restaurant employees began straggling in.

Carlita gathered her files and notes. She told Dylan to call her if he needed anything and exited through the back. Once again, Elvira's new company van was parked in the alley.

"Ugh." Carlita marched toward Elvira's back door and rapped loudly. It opened a crack. Elvira peered out.

"You need to move your van. You're blocking the alley."

"Right. I will." Elvira started to close the door, and Carlita shoved her foot in the crack. "Now."

"Fine. I'll move it now." The door flew open, and Elvira stepped out. "I don't know why you're being so nitpicky about my van. There's plenty of room to park at the other end of the alley."

"That's the point. You shouldn't be parking in the alley at all. It's a fire hazard."

"Whatever." Elvira rolled her eyes.

Carlita stepped onto her stoop. She stood off to the side and watched as her neighbor drove the nuisance vehicle to the parking lot.

Elvira climbed out. She slammed the door and tromped back down the alley. "Are you happy now?"

"Extremely," Carlita said. "Thank you."

"You're welcome."

Carlita turned to go inside.

"Hey!"

She turned back.

"The cops show up yet?"

"No."

"Good." Elvira's expression relaxed. "Maybe they're not going to."

"Maybe." Back inside, Carlita noticed the door to the pawnshop was ajar. She eased it open and found her son and daughter inside talking.

"You're back." Carlita joined them. "How is Shelby? What did the doctor's say?"

Tony cast his sister a quick glance, a look of concern etched on his face. "I was telling Mercedes...Shelby's diagnosis is more serious than we thought it would be."

Chapter 5

Carlita's heart plummeted. "Oh, no. What is it?"

"Shelby was diagnosed with Addison's Disease." Tony explained the disease was an uncommon disorder. "The doctor told us it can be life-threatening."

"Life-threatening? Carlita pressed a hand to her chest.

"Stress is a trigger. We have to be careful to keep an eye on Shelby's blood pressure."

"How...I mean what else did the doctor say?" Mercedes asked.

"He prescribed hormone replacement therapy. We'll definitely have a learning curve."

"I'm sorry, Tony. Shelby must be beside herself."

"She's taking it hard. Like I said, stress is a trigger. We need to learn how to de-stress her. She's putting in her notice at the post office. We agreed to take it one day at a time, but right now our main goal is to learn how to manage her condition."

A customer approached the counter, and Tony left to help them at the display case.

"I'm gonna go check on her," Carlita said.

"I'll go with you," Mercedes said.

They told Tony they planned to stop by the apartment, but he asked them to wait until later because Shelby was resting. "The news threw her for a loop."

"I imagine it did." Carlita waited until she and Mercedes were in the hall to talk. "This is terrible. I had no idea Shelby was this ill. I figured the wedding planning was the reason for her dizziness and exhaustion."

"And now she has to be careful about becoming stressed out," Mercedes said. "I wonder how or if this affects them and their future family plans."

"I don't know." Carlita made a mental note to bring it up to Tony when Shelby wasn't around, and they returned to their apartment.

While Mercedes headed to her room, Carlita began assembling the ingredients to begin making the chicken Milano. Her first step was to thaw a batch of her homemade fettuccine pasta.

While the pasta thawed, she added oil and the chicken breasts to a skillet. Mercedes emerged from her room and watched as her mother began combining the pasta, the sauce and the sliced chicken breasts.

"Something smells dee-licious."

"I hope it's delicious."

Mercedes patted her stomach. "It smells like something guaranteed to add to the beginning of my pasta pudge."

"Right, Mercedes. Like you have anything to worry about. It's a chicken Milano recipe. I'm testing it out for the restaurant." Carlita scooped a large spoonful of the pasta mixture on a dish and held it out for her daughter. "Give me your expert opinion."

Mercedes gobbled up the goodies. "I think I need another taste test."

"Which means you like it." Carlita placed two sample servings on small dishes and handed one to her daughter. She swirled the fettuccine around her fork and took a big bite. "I like it...nice and creamy."

"And absolutely dreamy," Mercedes quipped. "I think you should start by offering it as a dinner special and then add it to the menu if customers like it."

"Mercedes, that's a brilliant idea." The women finished their savory snack, and Carlita set the pan of food off to the side to cool. "We'll have this for dinner and maybe send some home with Tony so they won't have to cook tonight."

The outer doorbell buzzed.

"I wonder who that could be." Carlita reached for a dishtowel.

"I'll find out who it is." Mercedes darted out the door and down the steps. She returned moments later. "Hey, Ma."

"Did someone accidentally lock themselves out again?" Carlita hung the dishtowel on the front of the stove before stepping out of the kitchen.

"No." Mercedes stood in the doorway. She wasn't alone. A uniformed police officer stood next to her.

"Hello."

"Mrs. Garlucci?"

"Yes."

"I'm Detective Wilson from the Savannah Police Department."

"Detective Wilson. You look vaguely familiar."

"I believe we may have met while I was investigating a missing person's case."

"Ah." Carlita lifted a brow. "The JL Cordele case. Now I remember. How can I help you?"

"I'm sorry to bother you." The detective pulled a small notepad from his pocket and flipped it open. "I'm investigating the theft of a valuable painting from the *Darbylane Museum*. The owner of the security company hired to guard the artwork used you as a reference."

"Elvira Cobb," Carlita said.

"You know Ms. Cobb?"

"Yes, I know her. Not only is she a former tenant, but she's also my neighbor." Carlita motioned toward the alley. "She owns the building behind me."

"Yes, I noticed you two were neighbors."

"Unfortunately."

"I was hoping you could answer a few questions about your relationship with Ms. Cobb. How long you've known her, as a tenant had she ever done anything to cause you concern in a professional manner or otherwise."

"Ma evicted her," Mercedes said.

"Evicted her?" The detective plucked the pen from this front pocket and began scribbling. "If you don't mind me asking, why would you evict your tenant and then allow her to use you as a reference?"

"She didn't ask my permission to use me as a reference," Carlita said. "She just did it."

"I see. Could you elaborate on why you evicted Ms. Cobb?"

"It wasn't for theft."

"She set her apartment on fire," Mercedes said.

The detective's jaw dropped. "No kidding."

"It wasn't intentional; at least I don't believe it was intentional," Carlita shrugged. "The fire was the last straw, though. She probably shouldn't have used me as a reference."

"Would you have given her permission to use you as a reference?" Detective Wilson asked.

"I...maybe. Maybe not."

"There are two other local business owners Ms. Cobb used as references. Glenda Fox, the President of Savannah Architectural Society. Mrs. Fox is also Cobb's former employer, along with the owner of *Parrot House Restaurant*, Pete Taylor. Do you know either of them?"

"Yes," Carlita nodded. "Glenda and I are friends. Mr. Taylor is a business associate. I'm a partner in his pirate ship venture."

"Interesting." The detective eyed Carlita curiously.

"Savannah is a small town."

"It can be. Do you know anything about the missing painting at the museum?"

"I heard about it from a friend and also caught the local headlines about it this morning," Carlita said. "I'm not sure why someone would want to steal that particular painting."

The detective stopped writing. "You were at the museum yesterday during the exhibit?"

"Yes." A feeling of dread swept over Carlita. "I was."

"Did you speak with Ms. Cobb at any time during your visit?"

"I...Yes. Elvira offered me a 'behind-the-scenes' tour of the exhibit while waiting for a special guest to arrive. I took a quick tour of the museum, we stopped by the kitchen area to taste test some of the hors d'oeuvres and then we returned to the front."

"Did Ms. Cobb say anything about the exhibit, something which may have struck you as odd or out-of-character?"

"Odd? Yes. Out of character for Elvira? No."

"And what exactly was that?"

Carlita could feel her cheeks redden. "I...Elvira tends to make a lot of off-the-wall and odd comments."

"Specifically about the museum or the artwork?" Detective Wilson prompted. "Did she say anything about the artwork that was stolen?"

"Well..." Carlita hesitated. "Elvira dabbles in artwork, and she paints. She made an offhand remark about how her artwork was better than the artwork in the exhibit."

"Is there anything else?"

Carlita swallowed nervously. Although she'd told Elvira she wouldn't lie to the investigators if questioned, she was certain that repeating what Elvira had said - even in jest - would look bad. "Yes. She said she could replace *A Piece of Renaissance* with her own artwork, and that no one would notice."

The detective tapped the top of his notebook thoughtfully. "And it never occurred to you she might actually do just that?"

"No." Carlita hurried on. "You have to know Elvira to understand. She says stupid stuff all of the time."

"Yeah. All of the time," Mercedes chimed in. "It doesn't mean she actually does half of the things she talks about."

"I didn't take it seriously. Truth be told, I don't honestly believe Elvira is responsible for the missing artwork."

"Is there anything you can think of that you would like to add?" the detective asked.

"No," Carlita grimaced. "I think I've said enough."

"If you remember anything else, here's my card." Detective Wilson handed Carlita his card. "I believe it's time for me to stop back by Ms. Cobb's place now that I have this additional information."

Carlita held the door for the detective and followed him down the stairs. "Like I said, Elvira shoots off her mouth without thinking. I can't imagine her actually stealing the artwork. Besides, it would be stupid of her to take the painting considering she was in charge of keeping it safe."

Wilson stopped when he reached the bottom of the stairs. "You would be surprised at how dumb some criminals are."

Carlita waited for the man to step into the alley before slowly closing the door behind him. She trudged up the steps and joined Mercedes inside the apartment. "I don't think I did Elvira any favors."

"You didn't mean to throw her under the bus," Mercedes said.

"But that's exactly what I did." Carlita's mood was gloomy for the rest of the evening as she mulled over what she'd told the detective.

Obviously, someone had taken the painting. The number of suspects would be limited to those who had access to the museum and the painting.

Perhaps Elvira, in a moment of lack of judgment, had decided to "borrow" the artwork and planned to return it. Carlita quickly dismissed the thought. Pulling that kind of stunt would be damaging not only to herself but also to her investigative and detective services.

After dinner, Mercedes offered to run some plates of food down to Tony to take home.

While her daughter was gone, Carlita dialed Glenda Fox's cell phone number to let her know that Detective Wilson had stopped by. She planned to leave a message and was surprised when her friend answered.

"I was getting ready to call you," Glenda said. "The authorities picked Elvira up. She's being charged with stealing the painting."

"I'm not surprised. Unfortunately, I think I'm partially responsible." Carlita told her friend about her conversation with the detective, how Elvira had joked about taking the painting and suggested replacing it with her own artwork. "I told the detective she was joking, that you would have to know Elvira to understand she says and does some dumb things."

"She's in hot water now," Glenda said. "Elvira isn't the only one in hot water."

"What do you mean...she's not the only one?" Carlita asked.

"The authorities made a second arrest, and you'll never guess who it is."

Chapter 6

"A second arrest?"

"They arrested Dernice."

Carlita's eyes widened. "Elvira's sister?"

"Yep. Apparently, she was one of the security staff on duty yesterday and into last evening before the artwork went missing," Glenda said. "I'm not sure why they detained her, too."

Carlita started to reply and then promptly closed her mouth. She knew exactly why the authorities had decided to take a closer look at Dernice. The woman was a former convict, imprisoned in California for armed robbery.

She carried the phone to the balcony door and stared down at her neighbor's rear entrance. The place was dark. Carlita leaned to the side and peered down the alley where Elvira's new company van was parked.

"Elvira also used Pirate Pete as a reference. He knows a lot of the stuff that goes on around Savannah. He may have some information about the theft, too."

Carlita could hear a light tapping on the other end of the line.

"I feel kind of guilty," Glenda said. "I told the detective when Elvira was employed by SAS, she was always getting into trouble. I didn't mean to suggest she would actually steal a valuable painting, just that she was a pain in the rear."

"I pretty much said the same thing. I also feel somewhat responsible for the fact Elvira is taking the heat, and that Dernice is, as well."

"The authorities would not have arrested them unless they had some sort of proof they committed a crime," Glenda said. "Hopefully, Elvira keeps her cool during the questioning."

"That's debatable," Carlita muttered. "In the meantime, I think I'm gonna run by Pete's place tomorrow morning to see what he knows."

"Do you mind if I tag along?" Glenda asked. "We could have breakfast at *Garden of Goodness*."

"Sure." Before signing off, the women agreed to meet at the restaurant at nine the next morning.

"Who are you meeting?" Mercedes stood in the doorway.

"Glenda. We're having breakfast and then stopping by Pete's place to chat about Elvira's dilemma."

"Because you feel responsible," Mercedes guessed.

"Yes. I should've kept my mouth shut, and none of this would've happened." Carlita placed her cell phone on the counter. "Dernice has been detained, too."

"Because of her past record?"

"Yep. The authorities must've started doing a little digging around and found out about Dernice's criminal history."

Mercedes leaned her hip on the doorway. "Do you mind if I tag along? I'm working at *Ravello's* during the lunch hour, but I don't start my shift until eleven."

"Sure." Carlita changed the subject. "How is Shelby?"

"Tony said I just missed her. She was getting restless and decided to give him a hand in the pawnshop this afternoon."

"That's a good sign." Carlita stifled a yawn. "I think I'm gonna hit the hay a little early. Tomorrow is shaping up to be busy."

It didn't take long for her to get ready for bed. She glanced at the beam of light coming from under her daughter's bedroom door and could hear rustling coming from within.

Rambo beat Carlita to the bedroom. He flopped down on his doggie bed while she settled in with her remote and turned the television on. She mindlessly flipped through the channels before switching both the television and bedside lamp off.

Carlita fell fast asleep and then woke halfway through the night. No matter which way she turned, she struggled to find a comfortable spot. Finally, in the wee hours of the morning, she gave up and crawled out of bed.

Rambo gave her a quick look before flopping over to face the wall.

"I agree. It's way too early. Don't mind me."

She tiptoed into the hall. Mercedes' lights were off. She could hear the faint hum of the floor fan coming from her daughter's room.

After the coffee finished brewing, she carried a cup onto the balcony. The cool morning air gave her goosebumps, so she ran inside to grab a light sweater. Rambo plodded out behind her.

She settled onto the lounge chair and absentmindedly patted his head. What would Tony and Shelby do? Although Tony made a decent salary managing the pawnshop, Shelby's income helped pay the bills, too.

Shelby needed something to keep her busy, but maybe full-time was too much. Carlita tossed around the idea of talking to Tony and Mercedes about offering their new family member a part-time job.

The more she thought about it, the more Carlita warmed to the idea. Even if Shelby was a floater, helping in both the pawnshop and restaurant, it might give her enough to do to keep her busy when she was feeling up to it. It would also give the couple some extra money.

By the time she finished her second cup of coffee, Carlita was convinced her idea was perfect for all involved. Shelby and Tony could use the extra income. Carlita could use the extra help in a pinch.

"Hey, Ma."

Carlita jumped at the sound of her daughter's voice directly behind her. The coffee in her cup sloshed over the side and onto her pajama top.

"Sorry. I thought you heard me." Mercedes took a tentative step onto the deck.

"It's okay." Carlita reached for her napkin and dabbed at the damp spot. "How is the book progressing?"

"The words are flying off the pages." Mercedes flopped down in an empty chair. "I finally picked a name - *True Crime Mafia. Life in the Family.*"

Carlita wrinkled her nose. "Are you ever gonna stop writing about the mafia?"

"Yeah. This is the last one. My next book is gonna be a psychological thriller. I figure once Angelica Reynolds moves in, I can pick her brain."

"You haven't even spoken with her yet."

"I will. I have a good feeling about her."

"So what's the new story about...the one you're finishing up?"

"It's about a consigliere, an adviser to 'The Family.' He goes missing; the authorities suspect it was a family hit, but without a body, they can't pinpoint what actually happened to him. A decade after he went missing, the suspects in the case are found shot to death, execution style with the consigliere's initials carved on their right hands."

"A story like that would give me nightmares." Carlita shifted in her chair. "Why don't you write about women's romance or cozy mysteries...something that won't keep you up at night?"

"The only reason I'm up at night is because I'm writing. I have the stomach for the heavy stuff. I figure I can segue into thrillers," Mercedes said. "Besides, I gotta write what I know."

"Then we should find you a boyfriend so you can start writing romance," her mother teased.

"Very funny."

"Speaking of boyfriend, I wonder if Sam has accepted Autumn's dinner invitation yet."

"Who cares?" Mercedes popped out of the chair. "I'm gonna go get ready. We still on for breakfast at nine?"

"Yep."

Mercedes got ready first, and then Carlita hit the shower, her thoughts wandering to Elvira and Dernice's dilemma. Surely, the authorities had more suspects than just the sisters. There must also be some sort of video surveillance, which would help clear them of suspicion.

She finished getting ready and found Mercedes in the kitchen, a scowl on her face. "Did something happen while I was in the shower?"

"Sam Ivey."

"What did Sam do to annoy you this time?"

"It's not him. It's his dog."

"Sam has a dog?" Carlita changed direction and stepped into the outer hall.

Mercedes trailed behind. "It's a puppy. I took Rambo out while you were in the shower. We ran into Sam and his new companion in the parking lot. Did you give him the okay to get a dog?"

"Sam did mention possibly getting a puppy and making him his tour guide partner."

"Then we need to charge him a pet deposit and up his rent with a per-month pet fee."

"Mercedes," her mother chided. "I'm sure Sam is lonely. A puppy is a perfect companion. Let's stop by to meet him on our way out." She grabbed her purse before sidestepping her daughter and heading to the catty-corner apartment.

Carlita gave the door a couple of light raps. It opened a crack, and then Sam swung it open.

A brown puppy, his back dotted with white spots, scampered into the hall and pounced on Carlita's sandal. She bent down to pat the small pup's head. "Mercedes told me you got a puppy."

"Hey, there little fella," Carlita cooed. "He's adorable." She lifted her head and looked up at Sam. "What is he?"

"He is a she. She's a mix. I found her at the animal shelter. I haven't picked a name yet." Sam scooped the pup up, and she lunged forward to lick the side of his face. "She's a stinker."

Mercedes joined them. "Like dog, like owner."

Carlita shot her daughter a warning look.

"What?" Mercedes crossed her arms.

"Look at that adorable little face." Carlita reached for the puppy and cuddled her close. "You have little flecks of orange and brown. She reminds me of a..."

"Terrier," Sam said. "I'm going to make her my tour guide assistant."

"I love it." Carlita tilted her head and inspected the pup. "You need the perfect name. Something catchy."

"Piggly Wiggly?" Mercedes suggested. "She's got a little pot belly."

"She does," Sam laughed. "I was thinking of an old-fashioned name."

"How about Sadie?" Mercedes said.

"Sadie," Sam repeated. "I like the name...Sam and Sadie's Savannah Tours."

"Now that's alliteration. Sam and Sadie's Savannah Tours," Mercedes repeated.

Carlita shifted the pup. "Sadie?"

The pup let out a small squeak.

"I think she likes it, too." She handed the puppy to Sam.

"And I think we found a name. Thanks, Mercedes," Sam said.

"You're welcome."

"I owe you one. Perhaps you and Rambo can accompany Sadie and me for a tour of the area."

"If you're not too busy hanging out with Autumn." Mercedes clamped a hand over her mouth.

"Busy with Autumn?" Sam shook his head. "I helped her move. I would do the same for you and your mother."

"I think a doggie tour is a wonderful idea." Carlita placed a light hand under her daughter's elbow. "We have a breakfast date this morning, but I'm sure Mercedes and Rambo could fit you in a little later ...right Mercedes?"

"You're a tour guide. I'm sure you know all of the areas. You don't need me to show you around."

"True, but I don't know the hot spots for my new four-legged companion. I'm sure Rambo has some favorite areas."

"He does." Carlita eyed her daughter expectantly.

Mercedes clenched her jaw and gazed at her mother defiantly. "Fine. Yes. I think Rambo and I could fit you in our busy schedule unless you're working."

"No. As a matter of fact, I have a few tours this morning but took this evening off. Perhaps we could make it an official date, and I can take you to dinner," Sam suggested. "We'll call it a doggie and dinner date."

"I..."

Carlita was certain Mercedes was going to refuse and quickly cut her off. "Mercedes would love to have dinner and a doggie date. She'll see you around five then?"

"Yes." Sam grinned as Carlita took control of the conversation. "Five o'clock sounds perfect."

"She'll see you then." Before Mercedes could protest, her mother propelled her across the hall and down the steps. She didn't stop until they were on the back stoop.

"Why did you do that?" Mercedes slammed the door behind them.

"Because it's time you got it through your hard head that you and Sam have a chemistry. It's high time you stop treating him like a frenemy."

"We don't have a chemistry," Mercedes argued. "Besides, he likes Autumn."

"Says who?"

"Says me. He helped her move in. They're making dinner plans."

"Mercedes." Carlita wagged her finger. "That's absurd. He even said himself he would have helped us move, too."

"Yeah. Well..." Mercedes kicked at a pebble. "He was just trying to be nice. I don't think he expected me - expected *you* - to say yes to a date."

"I have to agree he expected you to say 'no,' but I'm also sure he's thrilled. You should've seen his face light up when you finally agreed." Carlita linked arms with her daughter, and they strolled to the end of the alley. "Someday you'll thank me for butting in."

"I doubt that."

Carlita changed the subject, and they began discussing the missing artwork. Both agreed they didn't believe Elvira or Dernice was responsible for the painting's disappearance.

"I'm hoping Pete can shed some light on the mysterious missing artwork. His pirate ship isn't far from the museum. He may have heard something from the guests about the theft. After all, both are popular tourist attractions."

They reached the restaurant. Glenda was already inside and seated at a corner table. She gave Carlita a quick hug and turned to Mercedes. "It's nice of you to join us this morning, Mercedes. I didn't think you were a morning person."

"I'm not, but I figured it wouldn't hurt to tag along and visit with Pete and Gunner. I guess he's expecting us?" Mercedes asked.

Carlita gave her daughter a blank stare.

"Pete doesn't know we're heading his way?"

"He does," Glenda smiled. "I talked to Pete last night, to find out if he would be at the restaurant or on his pirate ship. He's at the ship this morning."

A server approached. "Coffee?"

"Please." Carlita held up her cup.

The woman took their order. Carlita waited until she was gone. "The pirate ship adventures have been selling out. I wonder if business will slow now that the kiddos are back in school."

"We can all compare notes," Glenda said. "The *Riverfront Inn, Ravello's* and the pirate ship."

The food arrived a short time later, and the conversation drifted to Mark's *Riverfront Inn* and business at the SAS. After finishing their meal, Carlita insisted on picking up the tab. "It's my turn."

Mercedes and Glenda waited on the sidewalk while she paid the bill.

It was a short walk from the restaurant to the riverfront district. The skies were overcast, and a stiff northerly wind blew across the water.

Carlita shivered and tugged her sweater around her neck. "I'm not used to this chilly air anymore."

Mercedes rubbed the sides of her arms. "We're turning into true Southerners," she joked. "I don't think we could survive a winter up north."

"And who wants to?"

The trio reached the pirate ship. The gangway was down.

"Hello?" Carlita took a tentative step. "Anybody home? Pete, are you here?"

Heavy steps echoed on an upper deck, followed by a clambering on the stairs.

Pete appeared. "Well, shiver me timbers." A smile lit his face as he strode to the gangway. "If it isn't three fine-looking lasses come upon my merry ship."

"It's good to see you, too, Pete." Carlita gave her friend a warm hug before taking a step back. "You staying busy these days?"

"Business slowed down a tad now that fall is here, but not too bad. How about your new restaurant?"

"It's slower than I would like," Carlita confessed. "I have nothing to compare it to, so I was hoping you could ease my mind."

"Come on in. I'll show you what's new, and then we can talk shop."

"We're also here to see what you've heard about the theft at the museum," Glenda said.

"Well, now that, matey, is an open and shut case." Pete hooked his thumbs in his front pockets.

"They caught the culprit?"

"In a roundabout way you could say that. Elvira Cobb and her sister both confessed to the theft."

Chapter 7

"Confessed?" Carlita blinked rapidly. "You mean to say Elvira and Dernice are responsible for the missing painting?"

"It would appear so. I talked to a friend who works for the *Savannah Police Department*." Pete told them that the detective in charge of the case visited the women to question them a second time about the theft. "One of the sisters has a previous conviction."

"For armed robbery," Carlita said.

"Yes. She confessed to the theft, and then the oddest thing happened," Pete said.

"Knowing Elvira, it's hard telling what happened next," Mercedes said.

"Elvira confessed. She told the investigators she was the one responsible for the theft, and her sister was trying to protect her."

"They both confessed?" Glenda shook her head.

"Yep. Each of them claimed they were solely responsible, so the authorities arrested them both."

"I don't know what to say," Carlita rubbed her brow. "Why would they both confess?"

"Because they're both guilty," Glenda dusted her hands. "I don't feel responsible anymore, now that both of them admitted to committing the crime."

"I have to say I'm surprised. It seems out of character for Elvira to admit to anything," Mercedes said. "I guess we won't have to worry about her anymore."

The conversation turned to business, but Carlita only half-listened as she mulled over Pete's shocking news. Something about the confessions didn't ring true. Why would Elvira confess to stealing the painting? Obviously, she knew she would be a prime suspect not to mention her sister who had a previous rap sheet - for robbery no less.

Unless Pete was right...both sisters confessed in an attempt to protect the other one. Perhaps Elvira possessed a caring bone in her body after all.

Pete interrupted Carlita's thoughts. "I've done a little sprucing up around here. Would you like to take a tour?"

"As a business partner, I suppose I ought to," Carlita teased.

"And a pretty partner at that," Pete flirted.

Carlita could feel her cheeks warm. "No need to turn on the charm. I'm not trying to back out of our partnership anytime soon."

"Ah...you're a hard woman to compliment," Pete laughed.

"She can dish it out, but she can't take it," Mercedes mumbled.

"What was that, Mercedes?" Her mother lifted a brow.

"Never mind."

Pete motioned for them to follow him up the gangway and inside the main parlor where he pointed out a few of the changes he'd made to the snack bar. "I did a little tweaking to help with traffic flow."

He had also added a small indoor theater. "The theater is for the wee passengers who're afraid of the firing cannons and sword fights upstairs."

"That's a great idea," Carlita said.

They finished touring the main deck. Pete led them to the front of the ship and the captain's quarters where a full-size bed sat next to the swinging hammock.

"You're not sleeping in the hammock anymore?" Mercedes asked.

"Nah. These bones are gettin' too old to be sleepin' in one spot." Pete crossed the room to the back and the wall of rectangular windows.

"Gunner is great." Pete's parrot squawked.

"I didn't even see you there, Gunner." Carlita smiled as she approached Gunner's cage. "Are you behaving yourself?"

"Gunner is handsome."

"Yes, you're handsome," Carlita agreed.

Pete joined them. "Gunner has learned a new song."

"New song," Gunner echoed.

"Sing them your new song."

"Yo ho, yo ho. A pirate's life for me. I strut on my perch, watchin' the girls...the pirate's life for me."

"Bravo." Carlita clapped her hands. "I love the song, Gunner."

"Pretty girls for handsome Gunner," Gunner said. "Carlita is pretty."

"Thank you." Carlita shot Pete a quick glance. "I wonder where he learned that."

"I taught Gunner to appreciate beautiful women," Pete said. "A pirate's life gets lonely. I could use me a lovely lass."

Carlita fanned her face. "I'm sorry I asked. This conversation went right off the tracks."

"Ma doesn't get out much," Mercedes chimed in. "You two should hang out sometime."

"I like that idea," Pete tilted his head. "What do you say, partner?"

"Never mix business and pleasure," Carlita quipped.

"I think you two make a cute couple," Glenda added.

"How 'bout it, Ma?" Mercedes pressed.

"We need to find something else to talk about." Carlita changed the subject as they exited Pete's private quarters. They climbed the stairs to the open deck where Pete showed them a few of the other changes he'd made.

Several employees wandered down the sidewalk and began boarding the pirate ship.

"We've taken enough of your time." Carlita glanced at her watch. "We better let you get back to work."

"Thanks for stopping by." Pete followed the women down the stairs. "If you ever change your mind about a dinner date, lassie, you know where to find me."

"Yes. Thanks, Pete." Carlita gave him a quick smile, relieved when he turned his attention to the arriving employees. "We'll see you later."

The trio strolled away from the pirate ship, and Carlita playfully punched her daughter in the arm. "What was that all about?"

Mercedes smiled innocently. "What's good for the goose is good for the gander."

"You mean because I accepted your date with Sam on your behalf?"

"You said it." Mercedes nodded toward the ship. "I've seen it for a while now. Pete likes you. He's been waiting in the wings for John Alder to move away and out of the picture."

"I think you're wrong. Of course, he likes me. We're friends and business partners."

"No." Glenda chimed in. "He *likes* you. I noticed it at Tony's wedding. He couldn't take his eyes off you."

"Th-that's absurd," Carlita sputtered.

"We'll see," Glenda shrugged. "It wouldn't hurt for you to get out once in a while, even if it is as friends."

"Agreed." Mercedes waited until they parted ways with Glenda to speak. "What do you think about Elvira and Dernice's confessions?"

"I...it doesn't make sense. Why would Elvira destroy everything she's worked so hard to build over a painting she didn't even like?"

"We're talking about Elvira here," Mercedes pointed out.

"True."

"At least we can rest easy knowing we aren't responsible for helping put an innocent woman or innocent women behind bars."

Mercedes and Carlita made their way past the *Waving Girl Monument*, through *Morrell Park* and to *Walton Square*.

"I better get ready for work." Mercedes headed upstairs while Carlita stopped to check on Tony and the pawnshop. She found her son sorting through inventory in the back.

"Hey, Son."

He swung around before doing a double take. "Hi, Ma."

"How is Shelby?"

"She's okay. Thanks for sharing your pasta and chicken dish last night. Dinner was delicious."

"You're welcome." Carlita shifted her feet. "I've been thinking about Shelby and her job at the post office."

"She gave them her two weeks' notice."

"I have an idea I would like to throw out there." Carlita asked her son what he thought about having Shelby help part-time in the restaurant and the pawnshop. "It would only be when she's feeling up to it. That way, she can make a little extra money to help pay the bills, and she doesn't have to worry about working a nine-to-five job."

"That's a great idea, Ma. I'll run it by her."

"Perfect. Speaking of health, I need to give your brother a call to check on him and Brittney."

Tony thanked his mother again for the food and the offer of a job for Shelby, and she headed out the back door. She passed Mercedes on her way up. "Good luck at work."

"Thanks, Ma."

Carlita returned to the apartment. She dropped her purse on the counter and wandered to the living room window, overlooking the alley.

Had Elvira and/or her sister stolen the valuable artwork? Something wasn't sitting right. As if hearing Carlita's thoughts, Elvira emerged from the back of her building.

She hurried onto her balcony. "Hey."

Elvira trudged across the alley. "Hello, neighbor."

"I thought you were in jail."

"I was."

"Wait there." Carlita hustled out of the apartment and down the steps where Elvira stood waiting. "I talked to Pete Taylor a short time ago. He said both you and Dernice confessed to stealing the painting."

Elvira pinched the end of her nose. "The cops tricked us. I rescinded my confession."

"Did you steal the painting?"

"No. I thought Dernice did. I was covering for her. She can't go back to prison."

Carlita glanced over Elvira's shoulder. "Where is Dernice?"

"She's inside trying to find us a decent lawyer." Elvira explained the investigators picked the sisters up at the same time and took them down to the police department for questioning. "They interviewed us in separate rooms. The guy made it sound like they had evidence on Dernice. I didn't want her to go back to jail, so I kind of hinted maybe I was the one who took the painting."

"But you didn't."

"Nope." Elvira shook her head. "And neither did Dernice. They used the same sly trick on her, telling her I was on the verge of confessing. She was trying to save me from prison time, so she told them she may have had information about the theft."

"And they arrested both of you."

"Yep. When I found out what they were up to, I accused them of coercing a confession. I threatened to contact the local newspaper unless they released us."

"So they let you go," Carlita said.

"They had to. They have no evidence, and I was threatening to blow their cover. So now we're looking for an attorney." Elvira let out an exaggerated sigh. "You deal with the criminal element on a regular basis. I'm sure you've had to extricate yourself from a sticky situation or two. You got any suggestions on a good attorney?"

"I am not involved with the criminal element. I've never been to jail or prison."

"You're not missing anything. The food is disgusting, I was afraid to go to sleep and the cots are hard as a rock."

Dernice stepped into the alley, and Carlita waved her over.

"Hey, Carlita." Dernice nodded and turned her attention to her sister. "I found a couple of attorneys who might work. I told them I wanted to discuss it with you first."

"You get them on the cheap?" Elvira asked.

"Yep. One of them is fresh out of law school and looking to make a name for himself. When I told him who we were, he jumped at the chance to represent us. He mentioned something about holding a press conference."

"I wouldn't do that," Carlita advised. "You might say something you regret which could be used against you in a court of law."

"No kidding," Elvira grunted. "We need help, and we need it fast. The clock is ticking. It's only a matter of time before the investigators dig up something they can pin on me and Dernice."

"You're an investigator," Carlita pointed out. "Why don't you try to figure out who set you up?"

"I am. Don't think I haven't been working on it. I know one thing for sure. It was an inside job. During questioning, the detective slipped. I found out the museum's security system went down. It's as if the painting just vanished into thin air." Elvira snapped her fingers.

"Was the artwork still there when you locked up?" Carlita asked.

"Yep. Like I mentioned before, I had to run back inside. I forgot my keys when I was chowing down on some leftovers. Gaston Spelling, the museum's curator, waited in the hall while I ran back in to grab the keys. We walked out together. He locked up. We parted ways in the parking lot out back. The next morning, they discovered there had been a power outage during the night, and the painting was gone. End of story."

"You didn't notice any strange cars in the parking lot?" Carlita asked.

"There were lots of cars parked out back. The alley is used as overflow parking for some of the bars."

"I see." Carlita tapped her chin thoughtfully. "So the power went out, someone managed to get inside, steal the painting and exit the building without being seen or triggering the alarm. What about surveillance cameras?"

"The place is loaded with them. I asked Detective Wilson about it. He was very...how shall I say? Vague. It makes me think there was something going on with the cameras."

"Meaning they might not have been functioning at some point in time after you and the museum's curator left," Carlita said. "I'm sure the security system was on battery backup, so maybe for some reason, the system was down, along with the power."

"That would be my guess. Otherwise, they would have the culprit in clear view, and the alarm would have been tripped. There are surveillance cameras all over the museum."

Dernice, who so far had remained quiet, spoke. "I told Elvira we need to get back inside the museum to have a look around. There's some sort of storage area near the entrance to the museum. I noticed several of the museum employees going in there. We need to find out what's stored in that room. The only problem is that there's no way Elvira and I can pull it off without it looking suspicious."

"Dernice, you're brilliant." Elvira punched her sister in the arm.

"I am?"

"Yeah." Elvira slowly turned to Carlita. "*We* may not be able to get back inside the museum, but I know someone who can."

"Me?" Carlita's eyes widened.

"Yes."

"Oh, no." She began shaking her head.

Elvira clasped her hands. "Please? All you have to do is look around. The exhibit is open all afternoon."

Dernice joined in the begging. "You would be doing us a huge favor."

"I..."

"We need help. If not, two innocent women will go to jail for a crime they didn't commit," Dernice said.

A sly smile crossed Elvira's face. "I have a confession."

"Confession?" Carlita pursed her lips. "What kind of confession?"

"I...well, curiosity got the better of me. Not long after Tony and Shelby's wedding when the mafia guys showed up, I said to myself, 'Elvira Cobb, there's something to Vinnie Garlucci and his henchmen.' So, I did a little digging into the owners of the New Jersey casinos. Rumor has it that some of them are owned by the mob."

Elvira paused, letting her words sink in. "Your son, Vinnie, works for *Treasure Cove Casino*. In fact, according to their website, he's the manager of operations."

"Yes, he is."

"It's run by a mob boss, Vito Castellini. Correct me if I'm wrong, but Castellini is your daughter-in-law's maiden name."

"That doesn't make my son a mobster," Carlita gritted out.

"Nor does it make him a saint, so I did a little *more* digging around, up in New York. Queens, New York, right?"

"Yes, we lived in Queens."

Elvira decided to get right to it. "Your son has an arrest record, just some minor stuff - simple assault, disorderly conduct, discharging a firearm within the city limits to name a few."

"What's your point?"

"It would be terrible to think you've worked this hard to build your reputation and businesses only to have the *Savannah Area Restaurant Association*, of which you're a member, find out about your son's questionable character."

Carlita could feel her blood pressure spike. She clenched her fists. "This is extortion."

"Believe me, the last thing I want to do is damage your reputation, but we need help. You're forcing me to resort to desperate measures."

Dernice nudged her sister to the side and stepped between them. "We would never consider revealing your family's history. Elvira is talking smack. She would never throw you under the bus, but we could use your help."

Carlita tightened her lips and glared at Elvira.

"Please?" Elvira pleaded. "You know begging is beneath me. I'll owe you one."

Carlita softened when she noticed Elvira's eyes starting to water. "Well…"

Chapter 8

"Fine. I'll do it, but I'm not sure how much it will help," Carlita said.

Elvira grasped Carlita's hand, dragging her across the alley and into their apartment. "We need to make sure you're wired."

"Wired?"

"You know, earpiece, mini mic so we can communicate during the investigation."

"Oh, brother." Carlita wrinkled her nose. "This is not a full-blown investigation. I agreed to have a look around."

"And that's what you're going to do." Elvira didn't loosen her grip as she led her through the kitchen to the front and the offices.

Dernice trailed behind. "We have some extra sets in here." She began digging through the storage closet.

"This might work." She handed the equipment to her sister.

Elvira inspected the earpiece first. "This one is too small." She eyed Carlita's ear. "Her ears are too big. It'll get swallowed up."

Her sister handed her another piece. "What about this one?"

"This'll work." Elvira showed Carlita how to use the device and then tested the settings. "We're gonna have to stay in close proximity, not far from the museum if we want to maintain audio."

"I know the perfect place," Dernice said. "I'll show you when we get there."

"What am I looking for again?" Carlita adjusted the earpiece.

"A storage room. When you step inside the museum's front entrance, the ticket counter will be on your left, and the storage room is to the right."

"How am I going to sneak into the storage room if there's a person standing at the ticket counter in clear sight of the room you want me to snoop inside?" Carlita asked.

"That is a dilemma." Elvira rubbed her brow. "You'll need an assistant...err...accomplice. What about Mercedes?"

"She's working at the restaurant until early this afternoon. We'll have to wait until she finishes her shift." Carlita remembered her daughter's doggie date with Sam. "Scratch that. She's tied up all day."

"What about Annie from the real estate office?" Elvira suggested. "She's been with us on a spy mission or two."

"I can try to reach her."

"Hey." Dernice clapped her hands. "What about the new chick who moved into Carlita's building?

126

The young woman? I've seen her around before. Her brother owns the tattoo shop down the street."

"Autumn Winter," Carlita said. "She's helped out a time or two. I could ask her to tag along."

"She might just work," Elvira nodded approvingly.

"First, I'll need to see if she's available." Carlita made her way to the front sidewalk. Elvira and her sister followed close behind.

She began dialing Autumn's cell phone number but quickly disconnected the call. "I should try the *Savannah Evening News*' main telephone number."

Carlita searched for the number and pressed the "call" button. "*Savannah Evening News*. Gail speaking."

"Yes, I was wondering if I could speak with Autumn Winter please."

"One moment."

Background music played until Autumn answered. "Autumn Winter."

"Hi, Autumn. Carlita here."

"Hi, Mrs. G."

"I'm sorry to bother you at work."

"You're not bothering me. I just clocked out and was getting ready to head home."

"I have a huge favor." Carlita corrected herself. "Actually, Elvira, my neighbor, has a huge favor to ask."

"Elvira. Why does that name sound familiar?" There was a moment of silence on the other end. "I know why she sounds familiar. She was your tenant."

"And now my alley neighbor."

"She's the talk of the news department. I heard she worked at the security company in charge of the art exhibit. She confessed to stealing the famous artwork before changing her mind."

"She owns it...the security company, *EC Security Services*. It's kind of a long story. I'm at Elvira's place now. She and her sister claim they aren't responsible for the theft of the painting. They want me to have a look around the museum and a certain area in particular. I need a distraction."

"You want me to be your distraction?"

"Maybe. I would ask Mercedes to go with me, but she's working at the restaurant and has plans for later this evening. I'm not sure how long this will take."

"It won't take long," Elvira whispered.

Carlita motioned for her to be quiet. "If you're uncomfortable helping me, I completely understand."

"You know I'm always up for an adventure, Mrs. G. I'm in. When are we heading over there?"

"We'll leave as soon as you get here. I want to get this over with."

Autumn promised she was on her way and would be home shortly.

Carlita ended the call and waved her phone at Elvira. "I'll help you out this time since I feel somewhat responsible for your detainment. At the first hint of trouble, I'm out of there."

"You'll be fine." Elvira patted Carlita's shoulder. "All you gotta do is tell them you were looking for the bathroom and took a wrong turn."

"That's a flimsy excuse." Carlita sucked in a breath, already regretting her decision to help. "But I guess it'll have to do. I'll run home and wait for Autumn."

"Don't forget about us." Dernice followed Carlita through the building to the alley. "We're gonna be in the vicinity the entire time."

"That's reassuring," Carlita joked. "I'll swing by as soon as we're ready to go." She stepped back into her building, all the while wondering how the women had managed to talk her into participating in their snooping...and why she'd even agreed.

A breathless Autumn appeared on Carlita's doorstep a short time later. "Are we ready to get this mission underway?"

"I'm ready if you're ready." Carlita dropped the earpiece and mic in her jacket pocket.

Elvira and Dernice were already in the alley waiting.

"We can take the new company van," Dernice offered.

"No. We can't. Not with *EC Security Services* emblazoned on both sides. We'll stand out like sore thumbs."

"Elvira has a point," Carlita agreed. "We can take my car or walk. It's not far."

"I'm not walking," Elvira grumbled. "I get enough exercise standing on my feet day in and day out."

"The car it is."

The women strolled to the other side of the alley, and Carlita unlocked the doors. "I need to stop by the restaurant to let Mercedes know I'm leaving."

"Don't tell her what you're doing," Elvira said. "The fewer people who know what's up, the better."

"Fine. I won't tell her until it's over." Carlita dashed inside. She found Mercedes standing in front of the server station entering an order.

"Hey, Ma."

"Hi, Mercedes." Carlita peered into the restaurant's dining room. "How's business?"

"Pretty good, actually. The lunch special is our best seller. It's the Italian sub with a side of pinzimonio, the Italian-style crudites. I think we're onto something with these specials."

"That's music to my ears. I stopped by to let you know Autumn and I are heading to the museum. Elvira has convinced us to help her out, and Autumn agreed to be my distraction."

"Help her out?"

"I'll explain later. I shouldn't be gone more than a couple of hours." Carlita retraced her steps, giving the line cook and kitchen staff a wave before returning to her car.

She climbed inside and reached for her seatbelt. "Have the authorities talked to the man you were with the night the artwork was stolen?"

"Spelling? I don't know. I'm sure they have. I have a good instinct for people. I don't think he has anything to do with the missing artwork," Elvira said. "What about the artist himself? Abbott something. What if he lifted his own painting?"

"Why would he do that? He's in the business of selling, not stealing," Dernice argued.

"We can't rule out Elizabeth Portsmith."

"Who is Elizabeth Portsmith?" Carlita asked.

"She's some big shot loudmouth who has something to do with the historic district," Dernice waved dismissively. "No way."

"Portsmith is the Director of the Riverfront Historical District," Elvira elaborated. "I think she's cunning, crafty and definitely a suspect. She was watching the exhibit like a hawk. Every time I walked into the exhibit area, she was there with her old eagle eye on me."

"Interesting." Carlita consulted her rearview mirror before backing into the alley. "So we have three suspects, Roland Abbott, the artist, Elizabeth Portsmith, the director of the historic district and Gaston Spelling, the museum curator."

"Yep. One of those three swiped the painting," Dernice said. "I'm almost positive of it. They set us up."

"Except for Gaston Spelling," Elvira shook her head. "Like I said, I don't think he's responsible."

"We're still leaving him on the list." Carlita checked for oncoming traffic before pulling onto the street. "Now that Autumn is here, we need to go over exactly what you want us to do."

"Buy tickets to the exhibit. Autumn distracts the greeter/cashier while you sneak into the storage room. My gut tells me the painting is still inside the museum. Whoever lifted it plans to go back in to get it."

"What if they shoved it in their bag and carried it out the front door?" Autumn asked.

"Not possible," Elvira rubbed her forehead. "No one was allowed to bring bags inside. They were required to check them at the front desk."

"So maybe we should take a closer look at the greeter/cashier at the front entrance," Carlita said.

"Tabitha?" Elvira snorted. "That airhead couldn't fight her way out of a paper bag."

"I have to admit she was a bit of a scatterbrain," Dernice said. "But remember, she is kinda young."

"So we now have four suspects," Autumn said. "The greeter, the curator, the director and the artist."

"Motive and opportunity," Elvira sucked in a breath. "I'm putting my money on the hoity-toity director Miss Fancy Pants. Elizabeth."

"You're just ticked off because she got onto you," Dernice chuckled. "Man, you shoulda seen the look on your face when she caught you with the meatball in your mouth."

"It was ridiculous," Elvira muttered. "So I ate a tasty morsel or two."

"Or a half dozen."

"We're here." Carlita circled the block, driving past the museum before Elvira told her to turn onto a back alley.

"You got your earpiece and mic?" Elvira asked.

"Check." Carlita patted her pocket. "This shouldn't take long."

"Hang on." Autumn unzipped her backpack. She reached inside and pulled out a pair of stiletto heels.

Elvira curled her lip. "You're gonna break your neck in those things."

"That's the point. The shoes are my distraction."

"Ah. The old damsel in distress play." Dernice nodded approvingly. "I like it. It's both classy *and* crafty."

"Let's go before I come to my senses and change my mind." Carlita slid out of the driver's seat and waited for the others to exit the vehicle before locking the doors. She motioned to Elvira. "Where are you two going to hang out?"

"Well?" Elvira turned to her sister. "You said you had the perfect spot."

"Over there." Dernice pointed to a construction zone adjacent to the museum's parking area.

"A construction zone?" Elvira frowned.

"Close. There."

Carlita followed Dernice's finger and burst out laughing. "Now this I've got to see."

Elvira shoved a hand on her hip. "I am *not* hiding out in a porta potty."

"Do you have a better idea?" Dernice asked.

"No, but gross."

"It's the perfect spot. It's close enough to the museum for us to get reception. The work crew is nowhere in sight. Besides, I used it myself the other day, and as far as portable toilets go it didn't even smell." Dernice didn't wait for her sister and began making her way toward the lime green toilet.

Elvira mumbled under her breath and stomped after her sister.

Autumn waited until they were out of earshot. "Those two are a trip."

"Yes," Carlita sighed heavily. "You never know what's going to come out of their mouths next. Are you ready?"

"I am." Autumn took a tentative step in the stilettos. Her ankle twisted, and she faltered.

Carlita reached out to steady her. "I take it heels aren't your thing."

"Not at all. I bought these for a Halloween party last year. They've been collecting dust in my closet."

It was a slow hobble from the parking area, up the museum steps and across the porch to the entrance.

Carlita reached for the door handle. "Here goes nothing."

Chapter 9

Autumn tottered over the threshold and into the museum's front lobby. She kept a tight grip on Carlita's arm as she eased the door shut.

A multi-colored antique Tiffany lamp beamed soft yellow light inside the spacious rotunda, welcoming them inside.

"Good afternoon. Two for the museum?" The man behind the counter smiled.

"Yes." Carlita pulled out her wallet and handed him her debit card. "You're not busy this afternoon."

"Nope. The other day was a different story. This place was a madhouse. Everyone wanted to catch a glimpse of royalty. Half the town was here."

"I heard an earl or duke or some sort was on hand for the grand opening." Carlita watched him swipe her card before handing it back.

"Yes. He was here for maybe half an hour, tops. I caught a glimpse of the guy when he was leaving." The man pointed to Carlita's purse. "I'll need to hang onto your purse. We don't allow personal belongings inside the museum."

Carlita started to hand her purse to him and then snatched it back. "I can hang onto my wallet and phone, though."

He opened his mouth to tell her "no," but took one look at the expression on Carlita's face and quickly changed his mind. "Yes, ma'am. You can take your wallet and phone, but I'll need to keep your purse behind the counter."

She removed the items and held out her purse. "I think you're maybe going a tad overboard with the security. I'm sure there are cameras everywhere inside this place."

"When they work."

"We heard about the missing artwork, how the museum's surveillance cameras weren't able to capture the thief on camera," Autumn said.

"I...I don't know. That's the rumor going 'round, that there was some sort of power outage. It knocked out the security system and cameras."

A balding man, dressed in a three-piece business suit, entered the rotunda. The clerk snapped to attention. "Good afternoon, Mr. Spelling."

"Hello, Vance. I thought Tabitha was working this afternoon's shift."

"Yes, sir." Vance cleared his throat. "She asked if I would cover for her for a couple of hours. She had something to take care of first thing this morning."

"I see." The man turned to face Carlita and Autumn, a slow smile spreading across his face. "Welcome to *Darbylane Museum*. I'm Gaston Spelling, the museum curator. Is this your first visit?"

"Sort of," Carlita said. "I was here the other day. The place was packed, so I decided to return after the crowds died down."

"This is my first visit," Autumn said. "I've been meaning to stop by. When Aunt...Carlita invited me to come with her, I jumped at the chance."

"Enjoy the museum." The curator strode down the center hall, his heels clicking sharply on the gleaming marble floors.

Vance waited until he was out of sight. He handed Carlita two tickets. "The *Cotswold Georgian Exhibit* begins in the room to the left. Our permanent exhibit, *The River City,* is in the exhibit room behind the *Cotswold.*" He handed each of them a pamphlet, which included a detailed description of the exhibits.

They wandered into the first section. Autumn glanced over her shoulder. "Now what?"

"Keep your eyes peeled. I forgot to check out the storage room Elvira asked me to investigate."

Carlita crept across the room and returned to the doorway. She peered around the corner and into the lobby they had just exited.

She could hear Vance rustling papers at the counter and eased a little closer to the side. Carlita tilted her head to get a visual on the other side of the room. There, near the main entrance, was a smaller door.

Autumn scooted in behind her. "Is that it?"

"Yes. Now, all we have to do is create a diversion so I can sneak inside and have a look around."

"Let me think about it. In the meantime, we might as well enjoy the exhibits." Autumn led the way, and the women slowly circled the room. She pointed to an empty spot on the wall. "Is this where the missing painting hung?"

"Yep." Carlita nodded. "It wasn't very big. Someone could have easily slipped it into their jacket or with a large enough handbag, they could've placed it inside."

"Frame and all?"

"Yes, I believe they could have, except for the fact that no bags were allowed in here." Carlita's eyes slowly scanned the room as she counted the surveillance cameras. "None of these cameras were working when the painting went missing."

"It was an inside job."

"It had to be." The women finished their tour of the *Cotswold Georgian Exhibit* before making their way to the museum's permanent collection. "As much as I would like to appreciate art, sometimes I have a hard time figuring it out."

Autumn grinned. "You, too? I've been making a game of it, trying to figure out the artist's intent."

"Beauty is in the eye of the beholder," Carlita quipped.

"And worth is in the wallet of the collector."

"You said it," Carlita chuckled.

They circled the second exhibit area, *The River City,* and exited through a side door spilling into a spacious corridor.

Carlita recognized the corridor. It was the same one Elvira had used when she gave her the behind-the-scenes tour.

"Let's take a wrong turn." Carlita turned left instead of turning right - the direction of the front of the museum. Up ahead, she could hear the faint clatter of pots and pans. "This way."

They reached the butler's pantry, the spot where Elvira had sampled, and pocketed, a few of the tarts.

There was a swinging door on the other side and Carlita crept toward it.

"What are you doing?" Autumn hissed.

"Taking a wrong turn." Carlita swung the door open and stepped inside the bustling kitchen. The workers darted back and forth, taking no notice of the women.

High-end stainless steel appliances filled the large kitchen. The smell of fresh garlic wafted in the air. A woman wearing a chef's hat stood next to a butcher-block counter slicing bread.

Finally, one of the workers noticed the women and made his way over. "Can I help you?"

"Yes. I...my niece and I were wondering if you're taking applications. She's looking for a part-time job, and someone told us you were hiring kitchen staff."

"I...uh. The young woman's eyes slid to the woman standing at the counter. "Mrs. Finch might be able to answer that." She hurried to the woman's side and began talking in a low voice.

The older woman set the serrated knife next to the bread and wiped her hands before making her way over. "I'm Mrs. Finch, the head cook here. Someone told you we were hiring?"

"Y-yes...my friend heard it," Autumn stuttered.

"We may be hiring, but you're in no way ready to work in my kitchen." She pointed to Autumn's stiletto shoes. "I'll get you an application."

She reached inside a drawer and pulled out a clipboard before handing it to Autumn. "I have an opening for a dishwasher."

"Thank you. I'll take this to the hallway to fill it out." Autumn, along with Carlita, returned to the butler's pantry. "Now what?"

"I'm not sure." Carlita reached into her pocket. "Crud. I forgot to turn the earpiece on. Elvira is probably having a fit." She pulled the device from her jacket pocket, tucked the small earpiece in her ear and then turned the microphone on.

"Elvira, do you copy?"

"Yeah. Where have you been?"

"Sorry. I forgot. We toured the museum, stopped by the kitchen and now Autumn is filling out an application."

"Why did you go to the kitchen?"

"Why not? You told us to look around," Carlita said.

"There's nothing in the kitchen. What about the surveillance cameras?"

"The cashier, Vance, hinted the cameras weren't working during the time the painting went missing."

"Which confirms my theory the theft was an inside job," Elvira paused. "What are you doing?"

"I told you, we were in the kitchen."

"No. Not you. Dernice. Oh...do you have to do that right now?" Elvira groaned. "She's using the bathroom. Hang on. I need to turn around, so I don't have to watch."

Carlita could hear Dernice mumbling something, and then Elvira was back. "Have you checked out the storage room?"

"No. We're heading that way after Autumn fills out the application."

"Good luck. If you get a chance, snap some pictures."

Carlita promised that she would before turning the earpiece's volume down.

Autumn tapped the top of the clipboard with the tip of her pen. "This is a complete waste of time."

"Maybe. Maybe not. When we get back inside the kitchen, I'm going to see what the cook, Mrs. Finch, knows."

Autumn finished filling out the application and slid the pen under the metal clip. "This is as good as it gets. They would never consider hiring me. I have zero restaurant experience. There's no way I would take a job as a dishwasher. I hate doing my own."

"I appreciate you going along with all of this," Carlita said. "Elvira owes you one."

The women stepped back into the kitchen, and Autumn limped across the room. "I don't have much...uh...any restaurant experience."

"We can train if the right person comes along." Mrs. Finch perused the application. "You forgot to include your social security number."

"I'll provide it if or when I'm offered the job."

"Nope. I need it now. The museum runs a background check on every person employed here before they begin work."

"I'm not comfortable giving you that information," Autumn insisted.

"Then I'm not comfortable discussing a possible position in my kitchen." Mrs. Finch peered down the end of her nose.

"Fine. Let's not waste each other's time." Autumn stiffened her back and hobbled across the kitchen. She didn't stop until she reached the main hall. "I wouldn't want to work here anyway."

Carlita followed Autumn into the hall where she lifted her leg and began massaging her ankle. "These shoes are killing me."

"We're almost done. I need the diversion now if I'm going to attempt to have a look inside the storage room." Carlita's armpits grew damp. "What if we get caught?"

"You stick with the story you got lost. They can't do anything if a visitor accidentally gets lost."

"True." Carlita smiled grimly, a look of determination on her face. "I don't know how Elvira manages to involve me in her messes. I'm ready."

The women made their way back to the front. Vance was seated on a barstool, peering down at his cell phone.

Autumn squeezed Carlita's hand and began limping toward him. She slowly approached the desk. "I have a quick question about something in the gallery."

Carlita waited until Vance followed Autumn into the next room. She darted to the storage room, eased the door open and slipped inside.

The interior of the storage room was dark, and it took a minute for her eyes to adjust to the lack of light.

The room was filled with towering stacks of boxes, empty picture frames along with several pieces of small furniture.

Carlita moved quickly as she began rummaging through the boxes.

"It's no use." She gave up on sorting through the boxes and began a perimeter check of the room for a possible hiding spot. Carlita rubbed a frantic hand across her brow. It would take her hours to sort through the stuff.

Elvira may be right - the missing artwork was still on the museum grounds, but Carlita suspected it wasn't anywhere near this mess.

She tiptoed to the door and reached for the handle before remembering her promise to try to snap a few pictures of the interior of the storage room.

She eased her cell phone from her pocket and quickly snapped pictures from several different angles. Carlita switched the phone off and then gingerly eased the storage room door open, just enough to get a visual of the lobby.

Her heart plummeted when she spied Vance and the museum curator huddled in the center of the rotunda.

Autumn limped past them, carrying her shoes in her hand. She stepped outside and out of sight when Carlita heard her scream, causing a commotion on the museum's front porch. The men ran out the front door.

Carlita bolted out of the storage room. In one swift move, she pulled the door shut behind her. She darted to the entrance where she found Autumn seated on a wooden bench, her shoes on the seat next to her and clutching her ankle.

Vance and Mr. Spelling were both leaning over her. Carlita hurried to join them. "Oh, dear. Are you all right?"

"I took a spill on a slippery spot inside the museum. My ankle is killing me." Autumn blinked back tears.

Carlita peered anxiously at Autumn's swollen ankle. "You may have sprained it. I'll go get the car."

"If you could pull around to one of the handicap spots, we'll help her to the car," Vance offered.

"I need my purse," Carlita said.

Vance and Carlita returned inside while Mr. Spelling stayed behind with Autumn.

After retrieving her purse, Carlita hurried down the steps and to her car. She cast a quick glance at the porta potty.

The door opened, and Elvira emerged.

She motioned for her to stay inside before switching her mic on. "You'll have to stay put. Autumn twisted her ankle. I'm driving to the front of the building where an employee and Mr. Spelling are going to help her to the car. You need to stay out of sight."

"Ten-four," Elvira's voice crackled. "Swing back around the alley and pick us up."

"Will do." Carlita jumped into the car. She sped down the alley, around the block and to the front of the museum where she eased into an empty handicapped spot. Spelling and Vance helped a hobbling Autumn to the car.

"Thank you. Thank you so much. I...I'm such a klutz." Autumn hopped to the side and then backed into the front seat. She tossed her shoes on the floor.

"Are you sure you're all right?" A look of concern filled the curator's face.

"Yes. I'm sure I'll be fine."

"Thank you for helping us," Carlita said. "I'm sorry to be so much trouble."

"No. No trouble at all," Mr. Spelling said kindly. "You may want to leave the high heels at home next time."

"I will. Silly me for even wearing them." Autumn thanked the men again before pulling the passenger door shut.

Carlita climbed behind the wheel, gave the men a quick wave and backed out of the parking spot.

"Well? How did I do?"

"It was an Oscar-worthy performance," Carlita said.

"I was trying to fake a fall but ended up twisting my ankle instead. A little ice and I'm sure I'll be good as new." Autumn reached for her seatbelt. "Did you find anything inside the storage room?"

"No. It was full of boxes, empty artwork frames and furniture. It would take hours to dig through everything. Plus, I don't think the thief would be dumb enough to hide the artwork in the storage closet."

"Are you sure? It would be the perfect place to hide it...right in plain sight."

"I suppose. I took a few pictures. Maybe we'll be able to glean some clues." Carlita circled the block and returned to the alley before turning on the mic. "We're ready."

The porta potty door flew open. Elvira exited first, closely followed by Dernice. The women jogged across the construction lot.

Elvira hopped into the backseat and slammed the door shut. "I'll never do that again."

Dernice climbed in on the other side. "It wasn't that bad."

"It was disgusting. I can think of a million other hiding spots which would have worked."

"You're such a wimp," Dernice shrugged. "You need to toughen up."

"Well?" Elvira ignored her sister as she leaned forward in the seat. "Did you find anything?"

"I think I may be onto something, but it wasn't anything I found inside the storage area," Carlita said.

Chapter 10

"Like what?"

"Before I answer, what kind of information did you provide to the museum to get the security job?" Carlita asked.

"It was ridiculous," Elvira grunted. "The application was three pages long. They wanted so much unimportant information, I had to start making stuff up. Along with filler information, I had to include past employment, previous addresses, personal and professional references."

Carlita cut her off. "Who...did you use for a professional reference?"

"Well...uh." Elvira shifted uncomfortably. "I used Glenda Fox and SAS."

"With Glenda's permission?" Carlita pressed.

"I...was going to. I planned to, but never got around to it."

"Just like you used me as a reference?" Carlita pinned Elvira with a stare.

"We've already been over this. I was going to ask you, but I figured you would say no," Elvira whined. "It's not a big deal."

"Not a big deal? You're under investigation for theft, and you used me as a reference without my permission," Carlita said. "So now, not only does this throw suspicion on me but also on my family."

"It's not like you're not used to taking a little heat."

"Elvira." Carlita shook her head. She knew she wasn't going to win the argument and changed the subject. "Along with the references, did you provide them with a driver's license or social security number?"

"Yep to both," Dernice answered. "They required the information for each person who would be working security detail for the event."

Carlita's mind raced as she thought about Dernice's answer. "So...the museum directors and others would have access to your past conviction, Dernice."

"No." Dernice shook her head. "Elvira left me off the list. It wasn't until after the painting went missing that they started digging around and found out about my past."

"I think someone on the inside - inside the museum did find out." Elvira's jaw dropped. "Someone let us through, and gave us the job so they could lift the painting, and we would be blamed." She flung herself back in the seat.

"It could be," Carlita agreed. "We need to find out precisely who had access to your application. This might help us narrow down the list of possible suspects."

"I filled out the application online. A couple of days later, Gaston Spelling, the museum's curator, called me back."

"Then what happened?" Autumn asked.

Elvira told them that after filling out the application, Spelling contacted her for a face-to-face interview. "During the interview, Spelling told me I was in the running for the assignment. He gave me a stack of co-applications and told me each employee working would need to fill it out and return it within twenty-four hours. I didn't add Astrid's information since she wasn't an employee at the time I got the gig."

Carlita remembered the young woman who was learning French. "Why would Astrid's application be a red flag?"

"Because Astrid Herve is not her real name," Elvira said.

"We don't know Astrid's real name," Dernice added. "When we ran a background check on her, we discovered there's no Astrid Herve from Savannah."

"So she's hiding something." Carlita tapped the top of the steering wheel. "You said Astrid was saving up money to move to France."

"To get back to her roots, her ancestry," Elvira explained. "She's got it set in her mind all her dreams will come true when she reaches Gay Paree. She's a little on the innocent side."

"Gullible," Dernice added. "She sometimes strikes me as almost too innocent. Maybe it's an act."

"So maybe Astrid is a suspect in the painting's theft," Autumn said. "Where did you find Astrid?"

"Digging through a dumpster. She's homeless," Elvira said.

"Are you letting her stay with you?" Carlita asked.

"Sort of." Elvira averted her gaze. "Like I said before, Astrid - or whoever she really is - is a free spirit. She has anxiety issues and gets antsy when she's inside confined spaces with four walls. Astrid didn't steal the painting," Elvira said with confidence.

"Why not?"

"Because she never stepped foot inside the museum. Her detail was handling the outdoor crowds, something she's more familiar with."

Carlita had another thought. "How are you paying her if you don't know her name?"

"I think I mentioned it before. I'm paying her in cash and under the table. It's too much trouble to try to sort through paperwork when she's only a temp - and self-employed."

"I see." Carlita grew silent as she mulled over the new information. According to Elvira, Astrid was lying about her name. Maybe she had no anxiety about being inside buildings, but for whatever reason wanted Elvira to believe she had a phobia.

Why would the woman lie about who she was...unless she was hiding from something or someone?

"This makes no sense, Elvira. You're asking for trouble," Carlita said. "If Astrid lied about her name, she could be lying about her phobia of confined spaces."

"True. My gut says she's safe. I'm hardly ever wrong."

They reached the apartment building, and Carlita pulled into an empty parking spot. She waited until the others had exited the vehicle. "This investigative thing should be a piece of cake, Elvira. Just my two cents, but I think the theft of the painting was an inside job. Someone set you up knowing your employees, or at least one of them, had a criminal record, they stole the painting, and now you and your company are on the hook."

"It's beginning to look that way," Elvira said grimly. "I need to pinpoint exactly who at the museum had access to my application so I can narrow down the list of suspects. What about the pictures you took of the inside of the storage room?"

Carlita handed Elvira her phone and she silently studied the pictures. "They're dark and grainy."

"Because it was dark inside."

Elvira handed the phone back. "Thanks for trying."

"You're welcome."

Elvira and Dernice returned home while Carlita unlocked the back door to the apartment.

Autumn limped inside. "Do you think it was an inside job?"

"I give it a fifty/fifty chance," Carlita said. "I'm beginning to think they should take a closer look at Astrid. It concerns me Elvira doesn't know who she really is. She's lying about her identity which means if she's hanging around, we're going to have to be more cautious until we can find out the truth...figure out her real story."

Autumn lifted her injured ankle and hopped up the steps. "Do you really think she has a phobia of enclosed spaces?"

"I don't know. I have a feeling one day soon we'll know who she really is, and I'm not sure we're going to like what we find."

*****

Carlita helped Autumn pack a bag of ice and settle in on her sofa before returning home. She opened the front door. The overpowering fruity scent of peaches and lilacs filled the air.

"Mercedes?" Carlita followed the scent through the apartment and to the back.

The bathroom door was shut. She could hear Mercedes humming.

"Hey." Carlita rapped on the door. It flew open, and she stumbled back. "I need to buy a bullhorn and call you from a distance."

"Sorry, Ma. I didn't know you were home. I heard the pounding on the door and thought someone was trying to break in."

"Maybe because you write too many scary stories." Carlita tugged on a strand of her daughter's hair. "I love the ringlet curls. It softens your scowl."

Mercedes scowled.

"See? I was gonna remind you about your date with Sam, but I see you're already getting ready."

Her daughter impatiently swiped at one of the curls. "It's not a date. It's a non-date. Besides, this was your idea. I should make you go in my place."

"Sam doesn't want me. He wants you." Carlita critically eyed Mercedes' pale lavender button-down blouse and patterned gypsy skirt. "I guess the outfit will do. Why don't you borrow my diamond pendant necklace and matching earrings? It would look nice with your outfit."

"That's overkill. I'm not dressing fancy. Besides, this is the dog's date, not mine. I'm along as a tour guide so Rambo can show Sadie his stomping grounds."

"And have dinner," Carlita reminded her, the grin on her face widening.

"Stop gloating," Mercedes gritted out. "I spent all day at work trying to come up with an excuse to get out of this non-date." She tossed her hairbrush in the makeup basket and followed her mother to the living room. "Maybe I'll get lucky, and he won't show up."

"Oh, he'll be here," Carlita predicted. "My perfume is a nice touch. I haven't worn that in months."

"Not since your last date with John Alder, before he sold his place and moved away." Mercedes' tone softened. "Pops has been gone for a while now, Ma. Maybe it's time for you to get out there, too."

"Ah." Carlita waved dismissively. "I don't need to get out anywhere. I don't have time for men, for dating. I'm too busy. Besides, I'm set in my ways now."

"What about Pete?"

"Pete?" Carlita lifted a brow.

"Pirate Pete Taylor."

"What about him?"

"He likes you," Mercedes said.

"I like him, too."

"No, I mean he *likes* you. He taught Gunner to say 'Carlita is pretty - or maybe Gunner overheard Pete say it and is repeating what he heard."

Carlita's cheeks reddened. "That's ridiculous."

"Is it?"

Before Carlita could respond, there was a light knock on the door. She sprang to her feet. "Sam's here."

She opened the door. "Hi, Sam. Come in. Mercedes just finished getting ready."

Sadie let out a small *yip*.

"And look at you." Carlita bent down to admire Sadie's pink bow. "It looks like you're ready for your doggie date."

"She is, and so am I."

Mercedes joined her mother. "Are you sure you want to do this?"

"Yes. Sadie and I have been looking forward to our tour all day," Sam shifted his arm from behind his back to reveal a large bouquet of fresh flowers. "This is from Sadie and me, to thank you and Rambo for agreeing to show us all of the doggie hotspots."

"For me?" Mercedes' breath caught in her throat. She slowly reached for the bouquet. "I...thank you."

Carlita gazed at the orange roses, yellow sunflowers and gold chrysanthemums tucked in among an array of magnolia and autumn leaves. "You are so sweet."

"Thank you...Sam." Mercedes caressed the tip of one of the roses. "They're beautiful."

"I'll put them in some water if you two want to get going."

Mercedes carefully handed the bouquet to her mother. "Thanks, Ma."

"You're welcome." Carlita called Rambo to the door and waited for her daughter to clip his leash to his collar. "Have fun. Don't hurry back."

The smile was still firmly in place as she quietly closed the door behind them. Something told Carlita the relationship between her daughter and their handsome tenant had finally taken a turn.

Carlita hummed under her breath as she puttered around the apartment. She wondered how Sam and Mercedes' date was progressing, and then she began mulling over the list of possible suspects in the artwork's theft. Was it an inside job? Or could it have been one of Elvira's employees?

Tony stopped by after the pawnshop closed. "We're ordering pizza for dinner. Shelby asked me to invite you to come over."

"Thank you, Son. I was just wondering what to have."

"I figured we could discuss Shelby working part-time with us."

"Sure. Give me a few minutes to freshen up, and I'll head your way."

"Mercedes can come, too."

"She's with Sam."

"Sam Ivey?" Tony lifted a brow.

"Yes. Mercedes and Rambo are showing Sam and his new pup, Sadie, all of the doggie hotspots around here."

"You don't say."

Carlita motioned to the bouquet of flowers, prominently displayed on the coffee table. "He brought her flowers."

"Ah," Tony chuckled. "And Mercedes didn't punch him in the face?"

"No. I think she's finally coming around."

"It's about time."

Carlita promised to be along shortly. After a quick trip to the bathroom, she checked to make sure the back door was locked before stepping off the stoop.

There was a serene coolness to the evening air, and Carlita believed it was a sign that Sam and Mercedes were having a wonderful time.

She picked up the pace and strolled toward the opposite end of the alley. A bright beam of headlights bounced off the back of the building as a vehicle turned in her direction.

The car crept closer before coasting to a stop.

Carlita's eyes squinted as she attempted to figure out who it was. It finally dawned on her when she recognized the all-too-familiar vehicle, and her heart skipped a beat.

Chapter 11

Detective Wilson stepped out of his unmarked police car. "Mrs. Garlucci."

"Detective Wilson." Carlita greeted him with a curt nod. "What brings you to my doorstep once again?" Although she asked the question, she was certain the detective's visit was related to Elvira and the museum's missing artwork.

"I have a few more questions I would like to ask about the recent theft of the painting from the *Darbylane Museum*."

"Of course. I already told you everything I know when you stopped by yesterday."

"Are you sure you didn't leave out a few extra details?" The detective gazed at Carlita expectantly.

"No. Elvira used me as a reference. I know nothing about the theft of the painting."

There was a brief pause before the detective spoke. "Then let me refresh your memory." He removed a notepad from his front pocket and flipped it open.

"The museum's surveillance cameras captured you, along with Elvira Cobb, entering the museum via the rear entrance at approximately two o'clock p.m. the day the artwork went missing. Ms. Cobb accompanied you to the *Cotswold Georgian Exhibit*. You stood there for several moments studying the painting before the two of you returned to the hallway."

"Yes. As I explained to you the other day, Elvira was waiting for the special guest's arrival, so she took me on a quick tour of the exhibit. It doesn't mean I had anything to do with the museum's theft."

"Ms. Cobb is a suspect."

"Surely, you don't believe the person who was in charge of keeping the artwork safe is the same person who stole it."

"We have several suspects. No one has been ruled out." Wilson gave Carlita a pointed stare. "In fact, the museum curator claims surveillance cameras caught you sneaking into the storage room this afternoon. Would you like to explain what exactly you were doing?"

Carlita's heart sank, and her mind raced as she tried to come up with a plausible explanation for being involved in Elvira's dirty work. Even she had no sane reason for why she'd agreed to help. "I...was looking for the restroom and accidentally ended up in the storage room."

"You were in there for one minute and forty-nine seconds. I'm sure you must've realized upon entering the room that it wasn't the restroom."

"True." Carlita knew she was busted and decided to come clean. "Listen, Elvira did not steal the artwork. I did not steal the artwork. I told her I would take a quick look around, which is what I did."

"These incidents now put you on the list of suspects," Wilson said.

"It won't be the first time," Carlita muttered. "Elvira has a way of getting me in trouble without even trying. You're wasting your time. I'm an honest, hardworking business owner who also happens to reside in this community. I would be crazy to risk my reputation over a painting."

Detective Wilson motioned toward the apartment building. "Speaking of business...I hear you have an efficiency for rent. I'm in the market for a place to live. Since I'm here on a regular basis, maybe I should just move in."

Carlita lifted a brow. "To keep an eye on me?"

"Kill two birds with one stone," the detective smirked.

"Sam Ivey is already a tenant. One person with a law enforcement background is enough," Carlita shot back.

"Sam Ivey?" It was Wilson's turn to look surprised. "He's one of your tenants?"

"Yes and a wonderful tenant at that." Carlita consulted her watch. "If you don't have any other questions, I have a dinner date with my children."

Wilson tipped his hat. "I'm done...for now."

"That sounds like a threat."

"More of a promise." Wilson returned to his vehicle. Carlita watched him drive off before making her way to Tony and Shelby's apartment.

She climbed the steep steps and knocked on the door. Shelby peeked out before sliding the chain lock. "Hello, Carlita. Come on in."

Carlita gave her new daughter-in-law a warm hug. "You look good, Shelby. Are you feeling better?"

"Yes. I'm on medication now."

Violet darted across the room and flung herself at Carlita.

"There's my violet Violet," Carlita teased as she plucked at the child's ruffled purple dress.

"Nana Banana." Violet uncurled her small fist to show her grandmother a cookie crumb. "Mommy and I made cookies today. They're gooden free."

"Gluten-free," Shelby laughed. "They're chocolate chip."

Carlita inspected the brown smudge on Violet's pudgy palm. "Yes, I can see that they are."

Violet licked the spot and wiggled free. When she was on the floor, she slipped her sticky hand into Carlita's hand. "Tony and Mommy painted my room. Come see." She tugged Carlita across the kitchen, through the living room to her bedroom.

"This is lovely," Carlita admired the cotton candy pink walls before pointing to the prancing unicorns, smiling princesses and stately castles sprinkled across the top of the bedcover. "You have a new bedspread."

"Yep." Violet solemnly nodded. "I picked it out. Unicorns are real."

"And so are princesses." Carlita ruffled Violet's hair. "In fact, I think *you're* a princess."

"Now don't go telling her that. She'll make me her servant." Tony stood in the doorway, his arms crossed. "Thanks for coming by on such short notice."

Carlita turned. "Thanks for inviting me, Son. You've got this place lookin' like a real home."

The trio returned to the dining area where Shelby was setting the table. "Have a seat. The pizza should be here any moment. Can I get you a glass of lemonade or a soda?"

"I'll take a Coke if you have it." Carlita eased onto a chair while Tony helped his wife. Violet wiggled onto her lap. "Tony said you had something you wanted to discuss."

"Yes." Shelby gave her husband a quick glance. "We've been talking about…my recent health issues and work. I'll be bored silly sitting home all of the time. My job at the post office is going to be too much if I'm trying to reduce stress." She handed Carlita the soda.

"Thank you. So you think you would like to work here, with us?"

"Yes. I've never waited tables, but I'm a quick learner. I could pitch in wherever or whenever you need me."

"I like the idea. I think it's a win-win for everyone." Carlita sipped her Coke. "We need extra help. If you're able to be flexible, between the pawnshop and *Ravello's*, I think we can keep you as busy as you want to be."

They discussed Shelby's possible positions until the pizza arrived.

Tony set the box in the center of the table, and Carlita reached for a slice dripping with cheese. "This looks delicious. It must be Carmela's."

"It is."

During dinner, the trio talked more about the businesses, discussed the upcoming birth of Vinnie and Brittney's baby and then Tony mentioned Mercedes. "I can't wait to hear how Mercedes and Sam's date went."

"Her non-date." Carlita tapped the side of her packet of parmesan.

"Sam and Mercedes are dating?" Shelby smiled. "I thought Mercedes couldn't stand Sam."

"I suspect her feelings for him may have changed." Carlita told them Sam had adopted a dog from the local shelter. "She even took the time to dress up - well, dressed up for Mercedes, and she was wearing my perfume."

"Ah. She's got it bad," Tony joked. "Mercedes and perfume?"

"Well," Shelby said. "I think it's wonderful. All of the Garlucci children have found love."

Tony kissed his wife's cheek. "Yes, it appears that they have."

Violet made a gagging noise and wrinkled her nose. "Yuck."

Carlita chuckled. "Violet, maybe it's time to spend the night with Nana again."

"Really?" Violet bounced out of her chair. "Tonight?"

"Maybe not tonight but soon."

The family finished eating, and Shelby began clearing the table. She placed an extra slice of pizza in a to-go container.

"Thank you for the snack." Carlita leaned in to hug Violet. "Give me a day or so to get caught up, and then you can spend the night. We'll build a fort in the living room. You and Rambo can camp out."

"Can Grayvie come, too?"

"Yes, of course. Grayvie can camp out too, although I'm afraid he would be more interested in sleeping on top of the fort. I better get going. I'm curious to find out if Mercedes has returned from her date."

Carlita didn't mention it to Tony and Shelby, but she was also concerned about her surprise visit from Detective Wilson. Looking back, it hadn't been a wise move on her part to become involved in Elvira's shenanigans.

For the hundredth, maybe even the thousandth time, she asked herself why she felt sorry for Elvira.

She thought of the homeless woman, Astrid. Although Elvira could be a huge pain in the butt, she appeared to have at least one soft spot in her heart, however small it might be.

Carlita hugged Shelby good-bye. "Let me know when you're ready to begin helping out in the restaurant and pawnshop."

"I will."

Tony followed his mother to the door. "You want me to walk you home? It's pitch black out."

"Nah. It's only one building over."

"At least let me follow you to the alley."

Carlita carefully navigated the steep stairs. The overhead street lamps illuminated the narrow alley, casting shadows in the dark corners.

"You sure you don't want me to go with you?" Tony asked. "I don't mind."

"Nah." Carlita waved dismissively.

He turned to head back up the stairs while Carlita began cautiously dodging the dips in the gravel alley.

Ping. Her head shot up at the faint pinging sound coming from the direction of the parking area.

A shadow darted in front of the cars.

Burap. A chill ran down Carlita's spine at the sound of a heavy clanking noise. Someone was in the parking lot. She took a tentative step. "Hello?"

Her eyes squinted as she peered into the darkness. "Who's out there?"

Carlita slowly crept to the rear bumper of her car, and she had the distinct feeling someone was watching her.

She began backing up and had managed to clear the parking lot when a figure lunged forward, grasping a gun that glimmered under the streetlight.

Chapter 12

"Help!" Carlita shrieked in terror. She stumbled backward and lost her footing. The pizza container flew from her hands as she fell. A sharp pain shot up her back.

The shadowy figure flew between the cars and loomed over her. "What are you doing?"

"Tony!" Carlita screamed as she flung both arms over her head.

"What's going on?" Tony raced across the parking lot brandishing a gun. He aimed it at the intruder. "Hands in the air!"

The woman tossed the weapon on the ground and bolted. She collided head-on with Carlita's passenger side mirror and bounced off before tumbling to the ground. "Oof."

Tony dashed between the cars as he released the safety on his gun. "Make a move, and you're dead."

"I thought someone was trespassing."

"Trespassing?" Tony growled. "You're the one trespassing. I'm callin' the cops."

Carlita fumbled with her phone, her hands trembling. "I'm doin' it right now."

"You're making a big mistake. I'm a guest of Elvira Cobb. I'm staying with Elvira."

Carlita lowered the phone, eyeing the woman more closely. "You're...Astrid, Elvira's new employee."

"Yes. She told me I could stay here."

Tony kept his gun trained on the woman. "What are you doing wandering around in the parking lot after dark?"

"I'm not wandering around. I'm settling in."

"Settling in?" Carlita shook her head, confused.

"I have a tent. Elvira told me I could pitch my tent here."

"You're kidding."

"No. I'm claustrophobic in confined spaces, so Elvira gave me the okay to set up camp out here. Who are you?"

"Carlita Garlucci, Elvira's former landlord and neighbor."

"Oh...you're the mafia lady." Astrid rolled onto her knees.

"Mafia lady?" Carlita placed her hand on the back of her car and slowly stood.

"Elvira told me you have mob ties."

"Mob ties."

"Yeah. I think she was just kidding. She told me to watch my p's and q's or I might end up in the Savannah River with my hands tied behind my back and my heart carved from my chest."

"Oh, she did...did she?"

"Maybe she was trying to scare me." Astrid motioned to her weapon nearby. "You mind if I grab my weapon?"

"Yes, I mind." Tony took a step closer.

"I'll take it." Carlita scooped up the gun. "I'm hanging onto it until we can get to the bottom of this mess."

"I'll stay here," Tony said. "You go track down Elvira."

"I'll be right back." Carlita carefully made her way down the alley.

When she reached Elvira's back door, she pounded loudly. "Elvira."

She waited for a moment and then tried again. "Elvira! Open the door."

The door flew open. Carlita lifted the gun.

"What in the world?" Elvira flung her hands across her chest and jumped back. "What's going on?"

"This." Carlita waved the gun in her face. "I was on my way home from Tony's place, and your new tenant nearly shot me with this gun."

"Shot you? I...Wait a minute." Elvira reached for the weapon. "Give me that."

"Not so fast." Carlita thrust the weapon behind her back. "Whatever possessed you to let a homeless person - not to mention a person who is concealing their true identity - to pitch a tent in your backyard? Someone is going to get hurt."

Carlita could feel her blood pressure rising. "What were you thinking?"

"Chillax. You're making a mountain out of a molehill."

"*Mountain out of a molehill?* Astrid, or whoever she is, almost shot me. My blood would be on your hands."

"That's a stun gun. Not a real gun," Elvira pointed to the weapon. "I issue one to each of my employees when they're working security detail.

Even if she accidentally pulled the trigger, all you would've felt was a little sting."

Carlita took a closer look at the weapon. Elvira was right. In the dark, and at first glance, it looked like a gun. "A little sting? I'll show you a little sting." She tightened her grip and pressed the butt of the stun gun against Elvira's arm before pulling the trigger.

"Agh." Elvira's body began to shake. Her eyes grew wide; she let out a gurgled sound and crumpled to the floor.

"Elvira?" Footsteps clattered on the floor behind them, and Dernice appeared. She gazed at Carlita holding the gun. "You shot my sister!"

"Yes, and I enjoyed it immensely," Carlita said.

Dernice's eyes grew round as saucers. She dropped to her knees and reached for her sister's hand. "Hang on, El. I'm calling an ambulance."

"That won't be necessary. She'll be fine in a few minutes. I zapped her with one of your stun guns." Carlita held up the weapon.

"Elvira gave you one of our guns?"

"No. She gave it to Astrid, who pulled it on me while I was walking home a few minutes ago. She's out back with Tony who is holding the real deal. Someone has some explaining to do."

Carlita could see Dernice was torn between comforting Elvira and addressing the situation. She leaned over her sister and patted her shoulder. "Don't move...I'll be right back."

"I don't think she's going anywhere."

Dernice sprang to her feet and stepped over her sister's twitching body. "Did Tony shoot Astrid?"

"Not yet. At least he hadn't when I left."

Not willing to hand over the stun gun, Carlita shifted it to her other hand before motioning for Dernice to follow her.

They strode out of the building, to the other end of the alley.

Tony and Astrid stood under the lamplight. Tony's gun was still poised, ready to shoot while Astrid stood stock still, her back pressed flat against the brick wall.

"What happened?" Dernice asked.

"As I told Elvira, I was on my way home. I heard a noise and headed over here to investigate. Astrid pulled a weapon on me. I started screaming. Thankfully, Tony heard me. He ran down here. Astrid dropped the gun, and that's when she told us Elvira invited her to camp out."

"Yes, Elvira did," Dernice said.

"Someone should've told me," Carlita said. "I could've been hurt, and Astrid almost got shot."

"Elvira did tell you she invited Astrid to stay."

"When you said 'stay,' I thought you meant as a guest - inside your residence."

"I'm claustrophobic. Walls are too confining," Astrid said.

"I can't imagine a small tent is much better. Like I said, this was almost a tragic accident."

Tony lowered his weapon. "Astrid almost shot Ma."

"With a stun gun," Carlita said. "Elvira gave Astrid a stun gun to use when working security detail. It works quite well. I'm sure Elvira is starting to come around by now."

Tony's upper lip twitched. "You stunned Elvira with one of her own guns?"

"Yes. I was so ticked off; I reacted and gave her a dose of her own medicine." Carlita handed the stun gun to Dernice. "If I ever find out you injured one of my children, my family, I'll make sure the next weapon I use is the real deal."

Dernice's jaw dropped. "You would shoot us?"

"Either that or carve your heart out and toss you in the Savannah River."

Dernice and Astrid exchanged a terrified glance.

"I...I'm sorry, Carlita. This was all a big misunderstanding. I better go check on Elvira." Dernice took a quick step back before hurrying down the alley. Astrid ran after her.

Tony waited until the women were out of sight. "You got 'em going now."

"There's no sense in this." Carlita briefly closed her eyes. "Someone could have been seriously injured. Elvira needs to think first before doing whatever she darn well pleases."

"She might think twice now." Tony chuckled. "Man, I would've loved to see you nail her with the stun gun."

A small smile crept across Carlita's face. "I shouldn't have done it. It was the last straw. I finally got fed up with that woman. She's been a thorn in my side from day one, from the moment she moved in, to the time she set her apartment on fire to today when a cop showed up on my doorstep accusing me of being involved in the theft at the museum."

"Theft at the museum?" Tony asked.

"It's a long story." Carlita patted her son's arm. "Thanks for rescuing me."

"You're welcome." Tony tucked the gun in the waistband of his pants. "Let's check out the tent."

"Let me find my leftover pizza first." Carlita tracked down the pizza that had gone flying when Astrid surprised her. She did a quick inspection of the container to make sure it was still intact before joining her son.

The small domed tent was tucked next to the back of Elvira's building. In front of the entrance was a worn welcome mat.

Carlita's anger quickly faded as she gazed at the meager belongings inside...a backpack, sleeping bag and flashlight. "This is sad. Poor thing, living on the streets."

There was a small noise behind them, and Carlita turned. She watched as Astrid tentatively made her way over. "I'm sorry, Mrs. Garlucci."

"It's okay, Astrid. You need to be more cautious of coming after someone with a weapon. You might not be as lucky next time."

"I...I-you're right. Thanks for not gunning me down."

"We mafia-types only do that in the movies," Tony joked.

Astrid pointed to the door of the tent. "I don't plan on hanging around long. As soon as I make enough cash to buy my one-way ticket to Paris, I'm out of here."

"You're traveling light," Carlita attempted to lighten the moment.

"Yeah. I'm kinda used to roughing it. Life has been a little tough these past few months, but things are looking up. This is a temporary situation. Like I said, now that Elvira is giving me a place to hang my hat, I can focus on saving money and be on my way."

"And what about showering or meals?" A motherly concern filled Carlita. This young woman was homeless. "There's a women's shelter not far from here. I'm sure you would be much more comfortable at a shelter."

Astrid cut her off. "It's full. They don't have a spot for me right now. Elvira is letting me use her bathroom and shower. I know how to find food for free."

Carlita remembered Elvira's comment about how she found Astrid digging through a dumpster. "I own the restaurant across the alley. We'll be happy to share some leftovers with you."

"I..." Astrid began shaking her head. "I didn't mean for you to take me for a charity case. I can fend for myself."

"But we don't mind helping," Carlita said gently. "We all need a hand up once in a while."

"Well," Astrid shrugged. "If you got food you're gonna toss out anyway, I'll take it off your hands."

"Then it's settled. I'll talk to my kitchen staff about saving you some leftovers starting tomorrow."

"That'd be great." Astrid yawned loudly, not bothering to cover her mouth. "Whoee. It's been a long day. Elvira has a gig for me down at the boat docks first thing tomorrow morning."

"We'll let you get to bed, then. Have a good night, Astrid."

"Thank you, Mrs. Garlucci and you," Astrid motioned to Tony, "for not shooting me."

"This is my son, Tony. He runs the pawnshop." She told Astrid good-bye, and they made their way back to the alley.

"I'll walk you home." Tony offered his mother his arm as they walked to Carlita's apartment. She unlocked the door, and they stepped inside.

"What do you think, Ma?"

"I feel sorry for Astrid, but we must be wary." Carlita briefly explained what Elvira had told her, how she found the woman digging through a dumpster and offered her a job.

"Elvira was nice to someone?"

"Yes. There's something else. Astrid Herve does not exist. According to Elvira, the woman is lying about her identity."

"Maybe she's on the lam."

"It's possible. I had no idea Elvira was going to let her camp out here. She may be harmless, but you never can be too careful."

"You said it. I'll make sure Shelby knows what's going on."

"And I'll do the same with Sam, Mercedes and Cool Bones." Carlita thanked her son for walking her home. After he left, she locked up behind him and returned to her apartment.

The lights were on. She could hear Mercedes humming in the kitchen. "Mercedes?"

Her daughter popped into view. "Hey, Ma."

"How was Rambo and Sadie's date?" Carlita placed the pizza and her keys on the counter.

"It was all right."

"Just all right?"

"Yeah. Rambo and Sadie hit it off."

"What about Sam and Mercedes?"

"Don't look at me like that." Mercedes crossed her arms. "Fine. We had a good time. Are you happy?"

"Very," Carlita grinned. "So...are you going out again?"

"Maybe. I told Sam we should check out the *Pirates in Peril* pirate show." Mercedes returned her mother's sly grin. "Maybe we could double-date...you and Pete, me and Sam."

"There's nothing going on between me and Pete," Carlita shrugged her shoulders. "Don't be makin' something out of nothing."

"Whatever you say, Ma." Mercedes changed the subject. "Where were you?"

"Shelby and Tony invited me for dinner. Shelby quit her job at the post office and is going to work part-time at the pawnshop and *Ravello's*."

"That's a great idea." Mercedes plunked down on the sofa. "Sam knows someone who might be interested in a short-term rental of the efficiency downstairs. I told him to have the guy submit an application."

"I thought you had your heart set on the author."

"Angelica Reynolds. A man left a message earlier, asking if he could schedule a time to come by to look at the unit for her. I'm calling him back in the morning."

"Speaking of living arrangements." Carlita briefly told her daughter about her misunderstanding with Astrid in the parking lot.

"She's living in a tent?"

"Yes, temporarily. You must be careful. Her real name isn't Astrid Herve. She's homeless, and she has a stun gun...well, she *had* a stun gun. I'm not sure if Dernice gave it back to her."

"I will." Mercedes popped off the sofa. "You know what? Your run in with Astrid is awesome fiction fodder. I have the perfect place to add this scene to my book."

Mercedes returned to her room while Carlita put the leftovers in the fridge. Tomorrow was shaping up to be a busy day, and she decided to turn in early.

As she drifted off to sleep, Carlita thought about Astrid. What secret was she hiding? What was the real reason the woman was determined to move to another country?

She mulled it over before drifting off to sleep. Her last thought was the truth might be as unsettling as the incident earlier in the parking lot.

Chapter 13

Carlita's bed started to shake. Seconds later, the bedroom windows rattled. She bolted upright, clutching her chest. "What on earth?"

She flung her covers off and raced to the window while Rambo, who was curled up in his doggie bed, let out a low warning growl.

"You felt it, too?" She lifted the blind and peered into the courtyard. It was empty, but beyond that, she could make out the silhouette of a large tractor-trailer. Workers began unloading a massive bulldozer next to the vacant lot on the other side of the street.

The bulldozer rolled off the back of the trailer with another window-rattling thud. Rambo growled again.

"Great. Looks like they're gonna start building across the street." She lowered the blind and eyed her bed with thoughts of crawling back in until the earth shook again. "Third time's the charm. Guess that's our wakeup call, Rambo."

Carlita threw on some old clothes and headed to the kitchen to search for food she could give to Astrid.

The leftover pizza would work. She also whipped up a quick sandwich and placed that, along with some bottled waters and an ice pack inside a small cooler she found in the hall closet.

Rambo and she headed downstairs. Instead of letting her pup lead the way, she thought about Astrid and her tent and decided that until the two became acquainted, she had better keep him in check.

When they reached the patch of green grass, Rambo promptly investigated the tent and then patrolled the perimeter. She was surprised when he didn't growl or bark, and it dawned on her the tent was empty.

Carlita set the cooler on the mat and waited for Rambo to finish his business. They returned home where she settled in at the computer, first to check her messages. She sorted through the new ones, taking a quick look at a promising rental application and then noticed Glenda Fox had sent her a message. She double-clicked on it:

Mark heard from one of his friend's at the police station, the authorities are close to making another arrest in the museum theft.

Carlita's heart skipped a beat when she remembered Detective Wilson's surprise visit the previous evening. Surely, he didn't think she was involved. Yes, she had visited the museum with Elvira before the painting was stolen. And yes, the surveillance camera caught her sneaking into the storage area. Still, those two incidents weren't "proof" she was involved in the theft.

Glenda ended the message by telling Carlita she had an idea for *Ravello's* and promised she would call her later.

Mercedes joined her mother, who had wandered out onto the balcony, a short time later. "You're up early."

"You didn't feel the ground shaking this morning?"

"Yeah, but I ignored it." Mercedes lifted her hands in a slow stretch. "What's on your schedule today?"

"I'm working an afternoon shift at *Ravello's*. What about you?"

"I'm meeting Angelica Reynolds' rep to preview the apartment."

"What about the guy Sam suggested?" Carlita asked.

"I'm gonna hold off. I want to meet with this person before scheduling another showing."

Carlita sipped her coffee eyeing her daughter over the rim of the cup. "You really are determined to have this woman move in."

"Yes. I mean, this is the opportunity of a lifetime for me. She could help me fast track my writing career." Mercedes changed the subject. "I haven't seen much of Autumn since she moved in."

"She hurt her ankle yesterday while we were at the museum. Glenda sent me an email. Mark heard through the grapevine the authorities are close to making another arrest in the missing painting."

"Elvira?"

"Could be. She's having a bad week."

"I would say so. First the theft and then the tazing."

"I feel kinda bad about that." Carlita shifted to the side. "I blew my cool."

"Not a hard thing to do when it's Elvira."

"Yep. Glenda also said she had an idea for drumming up some business for *Ravello's*."

"Uh-oh." Mercedes leaned both elbows on the railing. "Check it out."

Carlita followed her daughter's gaze and then did a double take as a police car pulled into the alley. "Elvira's bad week might be getting even worse."

They watched Detective Polivich, another local Savannah detective, and a uniformed officer exit the car. Instead of heading toward Elvira's place, they made their way to Carlita's back door.

Her breath caught in her throat. "They're coming here."

"I'll go find out what they want," Mercedes said.

"No. You're still in your pajamas. I'll go down." Carlita handed her daughter her coffee cup. She darted inside and down the back steps to the alley.

"Good morning, Mrs. Garlucci."

"Good morning, Detective Polivich. I would like to say I'm surprised to see you this early, but maybe I'm not."

The detective reached into his jacket pocket and pulled out a piece of paper. "I have a search warrant to search your property and the premises."

"Search warrant? Whatever for?"

"*A Piece of Renaissance.* After further review of the museum's surveillance cameras, Detective Wilson and I obtained a search warrant for your place and for your neighbor's residence."

A second police vehicle, this time a large van, pulled in behind the patrol car. Several uniformed officers exited and joined the detective.

"Over there." Polivich pointed to Elvira's door before turning his attention back to Carlita.

"You...aren't going to search my tenants' units, are you?" she asked.

"We're searching your unit, your businesses and any storage areas."

"You're gonna be here awhile." Carlita thought about Mercedes still clad in her pajamas. "My daughter just got up. I need to warn her you're coming in."

"I'll go with you." The detective followed Carlita up the stairs.

"You think I'm going to hide something."

"I'm here to investigate. If you have nothing to hide, you won't mind me following you."

"Be my guest." Carlita marched up the steps and into the apartment; all the while mentally berating Elvira for her current predicament and the fact that the authorities were going to tear her place apart.

Mercedes was in her room. The detective followed Carlita to the doorway and stood off to the side while she knocked.

As per Mercedes' usual, the door flew open. Carlita didn't even flinch. She got right to the point. "The authorities are here with a search warrant."

"Here?"

"Yes. They caught me on camera at the museum, mistaking a storage room for a restroom. Now they want to have a look around our home and businesses."

"Elvira," Mercedes said.

"Exactly. So you may want to hang out in the living room until they're finished."

"Sure." Mercedes snatched her laptop off her desk and followed her mother into the living room, passing by the detective who was hovering in the hallway.

Two more officers stood in the doorway. Carlita waved them inside. "Let's get this over with. The sooner, the better."

The officers entered the apartment and began searching, all the while Carlita stewed over the fact that all of this was brought on by Elvira. Although she couldn't entirely blame her for the search. She did willingly agree to snoop around the museum.

She also couldn't blame Elvira for inviting her for a private tour the other day. Surely, Elvira had no idea the valuable painting was about to go missing. The more they searched, the more aggravated she became, convinced the theft was an inside job.

She remembered Elvira mentioning the museum's curator as well as the director. Was one of them responsible for the missing painting? The two had been involved in hiring Elvira and her team for the security job.

Could one of them have swiped the artwork and then pointed fingers at Elvira?

Carlita scowled at the officer who was digging around inside her desk drawer.

The detective and his officers finally finished searching the apartment. She met them at the front door. "Are you happy now that you tore my place apart and didn't find anything?"

"I'm sorry for the inconvenience," the detective apologized.

"Have you taken a closer look at the museum's staff? Perhaps this was an inside job. The fact the surveillance cameras happened to be off during the time in question is suspect. Certain staff members were given access to *EC Security Services'* application information and could easily make it look as if the security company or one of the employees was the culprit."

"We're covering every angle," the detective said. "We're even questioning the groundskeeper, Mr. Cagle."

"Groundskeeper?" Carlita asked.

"Yes. Mr. Cagle and his wife live in a small cottage on the property. They're getting ready to retire."

"I see. Now that you're done here if you'll excuse me, I have other matters to attend to." Carlita accompanied the officers to the lower level and into the pawnshop where several more men were wrapping up their search of the business.

Tony stood off to one side. She could see he was aggravated with the unexpected invasion. "I'm sorry, Son. This is my fault."

"My men are done searching your restaurant and pawnshop." Polivich joined them.

"Then let me show you the door," Tony smiled grimly.

Carlita waited for Tony to return. "I had no idea the investigators would show up on our doorstep to search the place."

"My guess is this has something to do with the missing artwork and Elvira."

219

"Your guess would be correct. Of course, they didn't find anything. I'm going next door to chat with Elvira."

She apologized to her son again and headed to the alleyway. The police vehicles were gone. Elvira's rear door was wide open.

Carlita stuck her head inside. "Elvira?" She could hear loud voices coming from the front of the building.

"Elvira." Carlita wandered through the back of the apartment to the front where the *EC Investigative Services* and *EC Security Services* offices were located. She found Dernice and Elvira staring each other down.

"I don't mean to break up a touching family moment, but I want to have a word with you."

Elvira turned, her eyes sparking as she stared at Carlita. "I'm still ticked at you. I was having hot flashes all night thanks to the zap you gave me."

"You told me I was making a big deal of nothing, that it was only a little sting."

"Yeah, well someone dialed the zapper to the max level. It was more than a sting. My whole body was on fire. It took hours for my nerves to settle down."

"Speaking of nerves, the authorities searched my apartment and pawnshop, thanks to you. Since you gave me a tour of the museum, and then they caught me on camera sneaking into the museum's storage area, they think I may be involved in the theft of the painting."

"Well, I'm in the same boat," Elvira whined. "If I can't clear my name, I'll never get another security job in Savannah."

"You need to take a closer look at your employees...namely Astrid. How can you be certain she had nothing to do with the theft? You don't even know her real name."

Elvira rolled her eyes. "I already told you. She never entered the museum. Her job was more of crowd control. She was familiar with the grounds."

"Familiar with the museum grounds?" Carlita asked.

"Yeah. Remember when I said I found her digging through the dumpster and offered her the security gig?"

"I remember," Carlita nodded.

"Well, it was right after Spelling told me I got the job. I was on my way back to the van parked behind the museum. I started to get in when I heard a clunking noise coming from the dumpster. I thought that maybe a stray animal was trapped inside. Instead, I found Astrid digging around, looking for something to eat."

"So she's been hanging around the museum." The more Carlita learned about the woman, the more she suspected that perhaps Astrid was somehow involved in the theft.

"Yes."

"I think Astrid is hiding something. She claims she's claustrophobic, but it could be a lie...like she's lying about her name."

Elvira tapped the side of her forehead. "I have a finely-tuned baloney radar. Astrid never even raised a blip. If she had, I never would've invited her to stay here."

"Just don't try to touch her stuff," Dernice warned. "She about bit my head off when I tried to move her backpack the other day. I thought she was going to come completely unglued."

"Another reason she may be involved. Maybe she has the painting hidden in her stuff." Carlita sucked in a breath. "I have an idea, but I need your help."

Chapter 14

"You need to give Astrid an assignment that takes her away from her tent so we can search her belongings," Carlita said.

"Bad idea." Elvira gave her a thumbs down. "She takes the backpack everywhere. I've never seen her without it. Not that I can blame her. All of her worldly belongings are inside."

"And maybe even a priceless painting."

"The cops already searched the tent. It was clean."

"We need to follow her, to see where she goes when she's not working," Carlita said. "What's her work schedule look like?"

"Let me see." Elvira stepped over to her desk and grabbed her day organizer. "She's working at the shopping mall out by the highway with Bif. She'll be there until nine when the mall closes."

"So we have plenty of time to search her tent." Carlita headed to the door. Elvira was hot on her heels.

"You got Astrid all wrong. Searching her stuff is an invasion of privacy."

"And so was having the cops show up on my doorstep with a search warrant and invade my private home." Carlita abruptly stopped when she reached the back door. "You don't have to go with me."

"Yes. Yes, I do."

Carlita marched down the alley. Elvira hurried after her. "I know you're upset. I can't say as I blame you, but none of my employees had anything to do with the theft. It was an inside job."

"We'll see." When Carlita reached the small domed tent, she unzipped the door and stuck her head inside. The tent was empty except for a sleeping bag, neatly rolled up. Sitting next to the sleeping bag was a flashlight.

She crawled inside the tent and unrolled the sleeping bag.

"This is crazy," Elvira mumbled.

"No. This is your fault." Carlita unzipped the bag and gave it a good shake.

"See? You wasted your time."

Carlita ignored her as she zipped the bag. She rolled it up and adjusted the ties that held the bag together. She carefully returned it to the same spot and dusted off her hands. "What time did you say Astrid gets off work?"

"Nine o'clock. Bif told me he would drop her off at the corner. Why?"

"Because I plan on keeping a close eye on her. I think you're wrong. I think there's a good chance she's involved in the theft. Think about it...how many times have your security gigs gone awry?"

"Well..." Elvira pressed the tips of her fingers together. "If you don't count the time Dernice accidentally tackled the mayor's brother during a scuffle at the *Riverfront Inn's* ribbon cutting ceremony, only once or twice."

"Tackled the mayor's brother? Never mind. What I'm saying is...all of the clues are starting to point to Astrid. She's outside security during the museum exhibit and only hours before the painting goes missing. She's lying about her identity. She refuses to let you near her belongings. In fact, Astrid keeps her backpack with her at all times. All of these sound like someone who is hiding something. If she can find a black market for the painting, she'll have more than enough cash for a first-class plane ticket to Paris."

Carlita backed out of the tent and zipped it shut.

"What are you going to do?"

"I already told you. I'm going to keep an eye on Astrid." Carlita had another thought. "Was Astrid around earlier when the authorities stopped by with the search warrant?"

"Yes. I mean, I saw her shortly before they showed up, but when they got here, she was gone," Elvira said.

"With her backpack."

"Yes."

"I rest my case." Carlita scooted between two vehicles, and the women returned to the alley.

"So you're going to spy on one of my employees."

"That's the plan."

"I want to go with you."

Carlita spun around to face Elvira. "Don't you care someone out there has set you or one of your employees up?"

"Of course I care. My reputation is at stake."

Their eyes met. Carlita stared at Elvira for a long moment. "My plan is to follow her this evening, whether you like it or not."

"Fine. I'll meet you out here at eight-fifty. I'll show you where Bif is dropping her off."

Carlita returned to the apartment and noticed Autumn's door was ajar. She could hear the tinkle of Mercedes' laughter and then her new tenant's laugh.

"Hello?" Carlita called out.

"Hey, Mrs. G." The door opened, and Autumn motioned her inside. "Mercedes was telling me about the search warrant."

"You missed out on all of the fun. I'm surprised they didn't get a warrant to search your unit, too, since you were with me at the museum. How is your ankle?"

"Good as new. Like it never happened." Autumn lifted her leg and rotated her foot. "They caught you on camera?"

"Sneaking into the storage room. They also caught me on camera with Elvira entering the back of the museum and touring the exhibit."

"They think you and Elvira are working together."

"Possibly. I personally think Elvira's new employee/yard guest may be involved."

"The woman with the tent," Autumn said. "Mercedes was just warning me about her."

"She's using a fake name. Elvira found her digging through the dumpster out behind the museum and offered her a job. She claims she's claustrophobic which is why she's staying in a tent. I think she's hiding something in her belongings, possibly the painting, and is using the claustrophobia as an excuse to keep her distance."

"What are you going to do?" Autumn asked.

"I'm going to follow her. If she is hiding the painting, she knows the investigators were here looking around, and she's going to have to make a move." Carlita told the women she planned to follow Astrid after a co-worker dropped her off later that evening.

"I'll go with you," Mercedes offered.

"It probably wouldn't be a bad idea. Elvira is insisting Astrid is innocent, and she wants to go with me, too."

"Are you sure, Elvira or even her sister, isn't involved in the theft?" Autumn asked.

"I'm beginning to wonder. This mystery is getting murkier by the minute. I do know one thing...I'm going to clear my name if it's the last thing I do. In the meantime, I'm going to give Glenda a call to see what idea she has for *Ravello's*."

Her call to Glenda went to voice mail. She hadn't even set the phone down when her friend called back. "You got my message?"

"I did. Believe it or not, the police showed up on my doorstep to search my businesses and my

231

apartment. They were looking for the missing painting."

"They think you're a suspect?" Glenda gasped.

"Yes."

"That's crazy. I wonder if they plan to search my place, too."

"I doubt it. I did something stupid. I helped Elvira, and it backfired."

There was a long pause on the other end of the line. "I can't say as I'm surprised...that helping her backfired, I mean."

"It's a long story," Carlita sighed. "So you have an idea for *Ravello's*, to help drum up more business."

"The riverfront district property owners are meeting today to discuss *Spooky Eats and Inns*."

"*Spooky Eats and Inns*?"

"It's a new tour some area business owners are putting together." Glenda explained the director of the riverfront's historic district was meeting with the locals interested in offering haunted tours of the restaurants and inns. "This would be perfect for *Ravello's*."

"I'm not technically in the riverfront district."

"But you're close enough." Glenda hurried on. "Your place was once a casket company rumored to be haunted. It would be the perfect place to add to the tour. Just think of the possibilities."

Carlita warmed to the idea. "I...yes. It might work. What an awesome idea."

"The director of the riverfront historic district, Elizabeth Portsmith, is holding a meeting at our place, *Savannah Riverfront Inn* in about an hour to pitch the idea to several of the inn and restaurant owners. I think you should come."

"It won't hurt to hear more," Carlita said. "I can use all of the help I can get."

"Then I'll see you in about an hour."

Carlita thanked her friend for thinking of her before disconnecting the call.

"Was that Glenda?" Mercedes stood in the doorway.

"Yes." Carlita repeated what her friend had said. "There's a meeting at Mark's inn on the river in about an hour. I figured I would run down there to hear what they have to say."

"I'll go with you."

Mercedes and Carlita made it to the inn with a few minutes to spare. Because of the large turnout, the group assembled in the enclosed courtyard.

Glenda's husband addressed the crowd and then motioned to a woman standing next to him. "I'm going to turn this meeting over to Elizabeth Portsmith, the Riverfront District's Historical Society Director. Elizabeth."

A tall woman, thin and with shoulder-length hair smiled at Mark before taking the mic. Her eyes scanned the crowd. "Thank you all for coming. After meeting with several of the riverfront business owners, we came up with a plan to offer a tour of the district's inns and restaurants. A haunted tour."

Elizabeth briefly outlined the idea. Carlita grew more excited by the minute. Her restaurant met all of the criteria with the exception of the location. Although *Ravello's* was close to the riverfront district, it wasn't technically on the river.

Mercedes tugged on her mother's arm. "This is perfect, Ma. Our place is haunted. It's close to the river. I think we should sign up."

"We'll see." Carlita didn't want to get her hopes up. Several owners raised some excellent questions. There was a detailed discussion about the nuts and bolts of putting a tour together.

Finally, Elizabeth suggested another meeting the following week and asked for a show of hands of area owners interested in the new venture.

Mercedes' hand shot up. "We're in," she whispered to her mother.

"I hope so."

"Perfect. We meet here next week at the same time. For those of you who raised your hands, please forward me your information and topics you would like to discuss."

The crowd began to clear out while several of the attendees approached Portsmith who was handing out business cards with her contact information.

Mercedes and her mother waited their turn before collecting the woman's card. She handed the card to Mercedes, but her eyes were on Carlita. "You look vaguely familiar."

"I own several businesses in *Walton Square*, including a new restaurant, *Ravello's Italian Eatery*," Carlita explained.

"Ah." The woman lifted a brow, eyeing her with interest. "You're also the one the authorities caught on camera sneaking into *Darbylane Museum's* storage area yesterday."

"It was a minor misunderstanding," Carlita mumbled.

"Uh-huh. Well, you're not technically in the riverfront district, so I'm not sure you meet the criteria for joining the tour owners. How did you hear about this meeting?"

"Glenda Fox and I are friends."

"I see. That changes everything. I suppose we could stretch the rules a bit." She pinched her thumb and index finger together. "I'm assuming the search of your premises didn't turn up anything."

Carlita shifted her feet. "No, it did not. I have nothing to do with the missing artwork."

"But you are a suspect," the woman gloated.

Carlita could feel her blood begin to boil. Portsmith was intentionally baiting her. "And so is every member of *Darbylane Museum's* board," she shot back.

"Thank you for the card. We'll be in touch." Mercedes grasped her mother's hand and propelled her out of the courtyard. "What was that all about?"

"You heard her. She practically came right out and accused me of stealing the painting."

"She didn't take kindly to your comment that she was a suspect, as well." Mercedes crumpled the business card. "It looks like we can kiss our chances of getting a spot on the haunted tour good-bye."

"Why?"

"You heard her. She thinks we're involved in the theft."

"And she has an ax to grind." Carlita's eyes narrowed. "I think it's time to take a closer look at Elizabeth Portsmith."

Chapter 15

Carlita texted Glenda, whom she'd seen at the meeting, but with so many people on hand hadn't been able to make it through the crowd to reach her. "We're outside on the steps."

A breathless Glenda joined them moments later. "Well? What do you think? Is the haunted tour something *Ravello's* might be interested in trying?"

"Yes, except that Ms. Portsmith doesn't appear particularly keen on having me or my restaurant join the group."

"Why not?"

"She doesn't like me." Carlita had a sudden thought. "Is Elizabeth Portsmith on the *Darbylane Museum's* board?"

"Yes. As a matter of fact, she is."

"We stopped to get her business card. She all but accused Ma of stealing the museum's painting," Mercedes said.

"You're kidding." Glenda cast a glance behind her, in the direction of Portsmith who stood talking to a group of business owners. "She's kind of a pain in the rear, but I can't imagine she would come right out and accuse you of stealing the painting when she's never even met you."

"She also seems to know a lot about the police investigation. She knows the cops searched my property this morning not to mention me being caught on camera snooping inside the museum."

"Snooping inside the museum?" Glenda smiled.

"It's not funny," Carlita said glumly. "Elvira talked me into taking a look around. The surveillance cameras caught me going into a storage area which prompted the cops to issue a search warrant and search my property."

"It seems as I missed a lot."

"Yeah. Lucky you."

"I wouldn't worry about Elizabeth. The business owners can override her decision. If you want to be part of the haunted tour, I'm certain the group would be more than happy to include you."

"Thanks, Glenda." Carlita eyed the woman over her friend's shoulder. "She's looking this way. Maybe she's the one who lifted the artwork. Motive and opportunity."

"The painting is valuable. Elizabeth would have plenty of connections. Opportunity is there. Perhaps the authorities are taking a closer look at her," Glenda said. "As far as Elvira, one of these days she'll get what she deserves."

"Ma evened the score with her last night," Mercedes said.

"She ticked me off, so I zapped her with one of her own Tasers."

Glenda burst out laughing, and even Carlita smiled.

"One of Elvira's employees pulled a Taser on me. When I called Elvira out, she told me I was making a big deal out of nothing - how it was only a small zap, so I made her eat her words. She went down like a sack of potatoes."

"I would've paid anything to have seen it." Glenda patted Carlita's shoulder. "Don't worry about Elizabeth. Like I said, if enough business owners are interested, you're more than welcome to join the tour."

"Thanks, Glenda," Carlita said gratefully. "And thank you for thinking of me."

"That's what friends are for."

Carlita and Mercedes returned home. The rest of the day passed slowly, despite Carlita working a shift at the restaurant. She kept one eye on the clock, waiting for Astrid to finish her workday.

Elvira was adamant Astrid was not involved in the painting's theft despite knowing the woman was lying about her identity.

Admittedly, there were a few holes in the theory Astrid was the culprit. She would have to be familiar with the layout of the museum. Whoever swiped the painting was either very lucky or somehow figured out a way to avoid being caught on the surveillance cameras.

How was it possible...unless - going back to it being an inside job. Someone knew something about the surveillance cameras, which helped the thief avoid detection. She remembered Elvira mentioning a power outage. Perhaps the outage was a part of the plan.

Carlita finished her shift at the restaurant with enough time to freshen up. At ten minutes 'til nine, she and Mercedes made their way to the alley.

Elvira was already waiting for them. "Right on time. This way."

They walked to the other end of the alley before turning right and making their way to the corner. "We wait here." Elvira eyed the vacant lot across the street. "They're finally going to do something with our neighborhood eyesore."

"Yes." Carlita gazed at the bulldozers ready to start tearing down the dilapidated structure and ramshackle fence. "They unloaded the dozers at daybreak. I thought we were having an earthquake."

"I wonder what they're putting in," Mercedes said.

"Hopefully, not another restaurant," her mother replied.

"We gotta clear the area so that Astrid won't see us." Elvira motioned for them to gather in the doorway of Carlita's corner storage unit.

Elvira, who was closest to the sidewalk, inched forward, just far enough to keep a visual of the street. The trio remained hidden for what seemed like forever, and Carlita shifted several times.

Elvira glanced over her shoulder. "You got a problem?"

"Problem?" Carlita shifted again.

"Ants in your pants."

"My feet are sore. I was working at the restaurant and have been on my feet for hours now."

"This was your idea," Elvira said. "I wouldn't be complaining."

"I'm not complaining. You asked me why I keep moving." Carlita closed her eyes and began counting, a regular occurrence when she had contact with Elvira for prolonged periods of time.

She smiled as she remembered the Taser incident and opened her eyes. "I see you've recovered from your small zap last night."

"Don't remind me. I owe you one," Elvira said.

"No. I owe you a dozen more zaps for the grief you've put me through."

"Shh." Mercedes held a finger to her lips. "I see someone coming around the corner."

"Astrid." Elvira's arm shot out. She nearly clotheslined Mercedes and her mother, forcing them back against the wall.

Carlita resisted the urge to bite her.

Elvira lowered her arm. "She's heading toward her tent." She motioned them out of the covered doorway as Astrid rounded the corner and turned onto the alley.

The trio tiptoed along as they followed behind.

"I see flashes of light. She's moving around inside her tent." Elvira grew silent. "The light went off." More silence. "It looks like she turned in for the night."

Elvira straightened her back. "See? I told you that you were barking up the wrong tree, wasting your time on a person of non-interest. Besides, it won't matter after tomorrow."

"Why?"

"Like I said before, Astrid only planned to hang around until she had enough cash to get to Paris. She told me earlier she has the money now. She made it sound like she was desperate for cash and would be hanging around for a while, but I guess not. She's bought her plane ticket and is heading out of town first thing Monday morning."

"Why not leave tomorrow if she's in such a hurry?" Carlita asked.

"She doesn't want to leave me high and dry after I helped her out and put a roof over her head. There's a festival over in *LaFitte Square*. It's a small one-woman job. She's covering until six tomorrow night."

"So she's staying an extra day to help you out," Mercedes said.

"Sort of. She also said she needs to take care of something before she takes off."

"Which means she takes care of this something either tonight or sometime tomorrow after work,"

Carlita said. "It will still be worth it to keep an eye on her."

"Suit yourself. Like I said, you're wasting your time. I have better things to do." Elvira left Carlita and her daughter standing on the corner.

"Maybe Elvira is right, and we are on a wild goose chase." Carlita stared at the dark tent. "We can't stand here all night."

"Wait a minute." Mercedes snapped her fingers. "I have an idea."

Chapter 16

"What happened to the portable motion detector we bought when we caught someone breaking into the pawnshop?"

"It's in our apartment, in the hallway closet," Carlita said.

"We can set it up on the balcony facing toward the parking lot. If anyone moves, including Astrid, it'll alert us."

"That's a great idea."

The women returned to the apartment. Mercedes made a beeline for the closet. She dug through several of the storage bins before finding the small, rectangular box. "I still have the app on my cell phone."

Mercedes tested the batteries and device before stepping onto the balcony. She placed the box in the corner, facing toward the alley in the direction of Astrid's tent.

"Now let's see if I'm able to get a visual." She fiddled with the front of her phone. "Success. Check it out." She shifted the phone so her mother could see the screen. "If there's any movement, the phone will chime."

They returned to the living room to wait.

Carlita turned the television on. She flipped through the channels while her mind wandered. She remembered the investigators' search of the apartment and properties.

How was it that almost one hundred percent of the time Elvira was directly involved in some sort of crisis surrounding her and her family? She set the remote on her lap and turned to Mercedes. "Do you think we should move?"

"Move? Why would we move?"

"To get away from Elvira. She causes us more grief than anyone I've ever met."

Mercedes laughed. "Ma, where would we move? This is our home. If anything, maybe you could offer to buy Elvira out and then evict her."

"That's a thought." Carlita mulled over the idea. She'd sold off almost all of the gems she and her children had found in order to get her businesses up and running. Now, all but *Ravello's* was turning a tidy profit.

She hoped that would change soon and *Ravello's* would surpass even the pawnshop as their primary breadwinner. She also made a small amount from her investment in Pete's pirate ship venture. The money was Carlita's "slush fund" for small projects.

With Shelby's health issues and her joining the family businesses, Carlita was even more aware of the weight on her shoulders in making sure her family and children were able to support themselves.

She sometimes wondered what Vinnie would think if he could see her now. She hoped he would be proud of her...proud of her not only for learning how to take care of herself after his sudden death, but taking care of her family...their children too.

Carlita had also worked hard to keep her promise to her husband on his deathbed...to get their children...their sons "out of the family." She had been successful in getting Tony out.

Technically, Paulie, her youngest, was never "in the family." Paulie lived in Clifton Falls along with his wife, Gina, and their three children.

Vinnie, on the other hand, was Carlita's biggest concern. Her eldest son not only had not gotten "out of the family," but he'd recently married Brittney, Vito Castellini aka "The Godfather's" daughter. Vinnie was in deep with the family.

Carlita was beginning to wonder if she would ever be able to keep her promise concerning their eldest son. "I need to call Vinnie to see if there's still a hit on Castellini and the family."

"I almost forgot about the hit. Vinnie brought trouble our way just in time for Tony and Shelby's wedding."

"I wish he was down here and not up in Jersey," Carlita lamented. "Your father is probably turning over in his grave and blaming me."

"It's not your fault, Ma. You've done the best you could. Vinnie is a grown man."

Mercedes' cell phone chimed. "We got something." She tapped the screen. "I can't tell who it is, but someone is on the move. They're coming this way."

"Let's go." Carlita tossed the remote on the sofa and scrambled to her feet. She grabbed her keys from the stand by the door and ran into the hall.

By the time they reached the alley, their target had already turned the corner and was walking at a fast clip. Mercedes and Carlita picked up the pace and began jogging to keep up.

The person stepped under the streetlight where Carlita was able to get a clearer look. "It's Astrid. Let's keep following her."

The duo stayed far enough behind to keep out of sight until Astrid turned right. "She's heading toward the museum," Mercedes said.

They jogged to the next corner. Astrid was still moving quickly, occasionally glancing from side to side. They followed her for two more blocks until she turned again, skirting a row of cars parked curbside and along the wrought iron fence that surrounded *Darbylane Museum*.

"She's heading to the back," Carlita whispered.

Astrid turned onto the narrow alley that ran behind the museum and then paused when she reached a row of dumpsters.

"Get back." Mercedes pushed her mother to the side of the building and into the shadows. They stood motionless, watching as Astrid approached the center dumpster. She turned around to check behind her before placing both hands on the top ledge.

Astrid heaved herself up, teetering for a brief moment before disappearing inside.

"She's inside the dumpster," Carlita gasped.

Mercedes pressed a hand across her mouth, waiting for Astrid to emerge. Several long moments passed before she popped out of the dumpster. She vaulted over the side, landing lightly on her feet.

"She has something," Mercedes said. "It looks like a bag."

Carlita watched in horror as Astrid unfolded the top of the bag. She pulled something out and shoved it in her mouth. "She's eating food from the dumpster." A wave of guilt washed over Carlita, ashamed of herself for suspecting the poor, homeless woman was a criminal. "This is terrible."

"You didn't know, Ma. Maybe we can do something to help."

"Maybe." Carlita had turned to go when Mercedes stopped her.

"Wait. Check it out."

A balding man dressed in a business suit approached Astrid. They stood talking under the streetlight for several long moments before the man handed something to her.

"He handed her something," Carlita said. "Quick. Take a picture of him...of them."

Mercedes lifted her phone and snapped several pictures. "It looks like he's handing her money."

"Why would a man in a business suit hand money to what appears to be a homeless person after dark? Wouldn't he be afraid of being robbed and attacked?" Mercedes whispered.

"You would think so." Carlita never took her eyes off them. "Unless...they knew each other. Watch their body language. This isn't the first time these two have met."

"You're right. We need to find out who this man is."

The exchange lasted for another few minutes before the man left. Astrid watched him walk away. She glanced at the side of the building before shifting her backpack and began making her way toward them.

"Hide." Mother and daughter dove behind a stack of storage crates.

Carlita's heart beat loudly as Astrid passed mere feet from where they were hiding. The women remained motionless for several long moments before emerging from their hiding spot.

Mercedes started to turn toward home, and Carlita reached for her arm. "No. I want to check out what's inside the dumpster. I have a feeling it belongs to the museum, and this is where the museum's café dumps their scraps."

Mercedes turned her cell phone's light on while Carlita hoisted herself up and peered over the side.

As she suspected, it was full of empty food boxes, to-go containers and scraps of food.

"Astrid was eating from the dumpster." Carlita hopped off the ledge and wiped her hands on the back of her slacks. "I left a cooler of food by her tent this morning, but there must be something more we can do to help."

"Let's go home." Mercedes turned to go when she caught a movement near the perimeter of the fence. It was a woman this time. She glared at them.

Carlita gave her a small wave. "We better get out of here. Looks like one of the museum's employees spotted us and is giving us the evil eye. She probably thinks we're the ones digging through the dumpster."

Back at the apartment, Carlita turned her computer on while Mercedes forwarded the pictures to her mother's email.

She opened the email and then they both leaned in for a closer look. "The man is handing something to Astrid. It's hard to see what it is from this angle."

Carlita studied his face. "He looks familiar."

"Check the museum's website. They may have a directory of the staff."

"Good idea." Carlita opened a new search screen. She typed in *Darbylane Museum and Estate*. The website popped up.

"There." Mercedes pointed to the top of the screen.

Carlita clicked on the *About Us* and then the *Museum Staff* tabs at the top. She began scrolling through the list of pictures and titles. She abruptly stopped, her heart skipping a beat. "Well...will you look at that?"

Chapter 17

"Gaston Spelling, *Darbylane Museum's* curator," Carlita read the description. "Autumn and I met this man the other day."

"And this is also the man we saw handing Astrid money."

"Maybe." Carlita flipped between the picture of Gaston Spelling and the grainy image of the man they'd spotted earlier talking with Astrid. "There are many similarities. Obviously, whoever it was came from the direction of the museum."

Mercedes peered over her mother's shoulder. "It's him. I would bet my life on it. Maybe he was being nice. He found out she's homeless and has been digging through the dumpster for food, so he's giving her money."

"At night, after hours and in the dark? It's possible, but I doubt it."

"Click on the sitemap," Mercedes said. "There, the exhibition floors."

The women scrolled through the screen. "There's nothing here."

"What about the gardens?" Mercedes asked. "We haven't scoped out the gardens yet."

Carlita clicked on the tab titled *Gardens,* but the page was blank. "I never thought to check out the grounds while we were there. After Autumn hurt her ankle and Elvira and Dernice were camped out in the porta potty, we took off."

"Porta potty?" Mercedes burst out laughing.

"You had to have been there." Carlita rubbed her chin. "I remember seeing a small cottage near the corner of the property. The cottage might be the groundskeeper's place."

"The woman who came out and scowled at us is the groundskeeper? I'm sure they're spooked, what with the theft, not to mention Astrid hanging around there all of the time." Mercedes had a thought. "Go back to the *Museum Staff*. Is there any information about a groundskeeper?"

Carlita clicked on the link. At the bottom of the list was a picture of a man, Henry Cagle, Caretaker. "Henry Cagle." Next to the man's photo was a picture of a gray-haired woman, a solemn expression on her face. "Mabel Cagle. These are the caretakers. I think this is the woman who was standing next to the fence scowling at us."

"Yes," Mercedes agreed. "That's her. I recognize the look on her face. So now what?"

"I'm thinkin'." Carlita drummed her fingers on the desk. "I'm thinkin' something fishy is going on at the museum. They hired Elvira and *EC Security Services* for the exhibit event...and on the busiest day, after everyone leaves, the valuable painting goes missing. Dernice has a criminal record. Even if

Elvira 'fudged' the information and didn't mention Dernice, something is off."

"And it doesn't help that you were there sneaking in the back with Elvira, not to mention being caught on camera sneaking into the storage area," Mercedes pointed out.

"Dummy me. It was a stupid move on my part," Carlita said. "Now look at the mess we're in."

"Don't beat yourself up too badly, Ma."

"If I get out of this mess, mark my words...it won't happen again. Back to the missing artwork. Here comes Astrid, hired by Elvira, who knows the woman is lying about her identity. In fact, Elvira meets her after finding her digging around inside the dumpster behind the museum. We follow her back to the museum. She's scrounging around for something to eat despite me leaving food for her. A man we suspect may be the museum's curator hands her something."

"I agree...you may be onto something," Mercedes said.

Carlita swiveled around. "Astrid isn't letting her backpack out of her sight. Dernice even made a comment about how when she tried to move it, Astrid flew off the handle and freaked out."

"How large is the missing artwork?" Mercedes asked.

"About this big." Carlita held her hands out. "It's small enough to fit inside a backpack."

"So you think Astrid has the artwork." Mercedes began to pace. "What if she stole the artwork for someone working at the museum and is hanging onto it until the heat is off? She turns it over to whoever she's working for in exchange..."

"...for money," Carlita and Mercedes said in unison.

"There's a reason Astrid is hanging around the museum. We need to get our hands on her backpack."

"But how? You said it never leaves her side," Mercedes said.

"I'm going to do some thinking on that. If Astrid is responsible for swiping the painting, she has an accomplice - someone who knows the value of the painting and may even have black market connections to sell it once the investigation dies down."

"An employee, someone who works at the museum."

Carlita reached for a yellow pad of paper and pen. "We need to make a list of suspects." She scribbled *A Piece of Renaissance Suspects* at the top of the page. "At the top of the list is Astrid. She's lying; she's hiding something and keeps returning to the museum."

"Next would be the museum curator...the man we saw handing something to Astrid."

"Right." Carlita wrote his name below Astrid's and consulted the staff list. "This woman, Elizabeth

Portsmith, Director of Riverfront Historical Society. The one we met earlier today who coincidentally knows a whole lot about the police investigation."

"She does," Mercedes agreed. "Wouldn't that be something?"

"Yes, it would." Carlita added her name to the list. "Elvira also mentioned a young woman who was working the front desk, checking bags the day of the big event. She would have access to anyone and everyone's personal belongings, perhaps even the thief's belongings."

"Would you consider her a suspect?" Mercedes asked.

"I would, considering she had access to visitors' belongings and certain areas of the museum, at least during the daytime hours. Suspect the least suspect."

"Not to mention motive and opportunity. All four of them had motive and opportunity...Astrid,

Gaston Spelling, the Portsmith lady. I guess we should include the clerk, too."

"And Elvira/Dernice." Carlita drew a fill-in-the-blank line for the employee's name and then added the sisters' names. "They would have to be clever, not to mention lucky, to get the painting off the premises."

"Which is why the woman who was working that day is also a suspect. She could be an accomplice, returning after hours to help swipe the painting."

Mercedes tapped her mother's arm. "What if the painting hasn't left the premises? What if it's still there...somewhere?"

"Elvira suggested the same thing." Carlita shifted her gaze, staring sightlessly out the French doors. "We need someone to go back in, to visit the museum and the grounds. I can't do it. Autumn is off the list."

"But I'm not," Mercedes said. "I could run over there and have a look around."

"No." Carlita dismissed the suggestion. "I think it should be someone else."

"What about Tony and Shelby? We could offer to watch the pawnshop tomorrow for a few hours while they take Violet to the museum. No one would look twice at a couple with a young child if they say...wandered into restricted areas."

"That's a great idea, Mercedes. No one would ever suspect a nice little family of snooping around. Now, all we have to do is get Tony onboard."

Before heading to bed, Carlita sent a text message to Tony's cell phone to ask if Shelby was going to be home tomorrow. He replied that she was.

Carlita told him she had a special favor to ask in the morning and it involved Shelby and Violet. She ended the text reply by telling him she would see him in the morning.

She switched her cell phone off and set it on the nightstand before turning off her bedroom lamp. It took hours for her to fall asleep. She thought about

Astrid, wondering if the woman was involved in the painting's theft. If she was in it for cash, perhaps she had been key in securing the painting in exchange for a large sum of money...enough to buy her plane ticket to Paris.

There was something to the backpack. Perhaps Carlita should alert the authorities to her suspicions, and then they could search Astrid's belongings, but even a simple search would require a warrant.

There was another conundrum...what would she tell the authorities? She was following the woman around, found her digging in the dumpster behind the museum and saw a man hand her something?

They would wonder why Carlita was following her. She was already a suspect. She tossed and turned, torn between contacting Detective Wilson and Detective Polivich and running the risk of heaping even more suspicion on her head - or hold off until she had a better idea if Elvira's employee was involved.

She finally decided to wait until Tony, Shelby and Violet finished their tour of the museum and gardens before making a decision.

Perhaps then, she would have a better idea of how someone could've pulled off the theft, giving her a clearer picture of what may have happened.

With a decision made, Carlita finally drifted off to sleep...now all she had to do was convince Tony to go along with her plan.

*****

"I don't think this is such a good idea," Tony shook his head. "The cops are hot on the case. Polivich and his men were in here the other day tearing this place apart. If we show up at the museum, they're going to think something is up."

"I disagree. Besides, it's not against the law to visit a museum," Carlita said.

"What's wrong with a cozy little family outing?" Mercedes chimed in. "The gardens look lovely."

"I would like to go, Tony. Your mother is right. We're not committing a crime by visiting the museum," Shelby said.

"They even have a café on the grounds. You could visit the museum, the gardens and have lunch," Carlita enticed.

"I want to go." Violet hopped up and down on one foot as she tugged on Tony's hand.

He chuckled. "You want to look at a bunch of boring old paintings?"

"And pretty flowers," Shelby added.

The couples' eyes met, which was all it took for Tony to cave. "Fine. We'll go, but don't ask me to sneak into backrooms and stuff."

"I wouldn't dream of it. We need someone to take a closer look at the grounds," Carlita beamed. "Reese and the trolley will be along shortly. If you leave now, you'll have enough time to grab your things and head out."

She followed her son and his family to the door. "Don't worry about us. It's good for Mercedes and me to handle business around here and give you a break."

"Are you sure?" Tony's steps slowed.

"I promise." Carlita nudged him toward the door. "We'll be fine." She waited until they were gone and the door was shut. "That was harder than I thought it would be."

"Tony doesn't like to leave the pawnshop," Mercedes said. "I'm surprised he didn't try to convince Shelby to move into his bachelor pad so he could stay close to this place."

"Speaking of bachelor pad, any news on the potential writer tenant?"

"Her agent is stopping by today to tour the unit."

A customer walked in interrupting the conversation. The morning passed by quickly while Carlita kept a keen eye on the clock. The museum wasn't large and the gardens, although sprawling, wouldn't take long to tour.

Mercedes joined her mother near the back of the store. "You're wondering what happened to them."

"Yeah. I figured the visit would take a coupla hours, tops."

"They were also going to have lunch," Mercedes pointed out.

"True. As long as they're enjoying themselves, I guess I shouldn't worry."

A young man stepped into the pawnshop and approached the counter. "Hello. I'm here to meet with someone to tour an efficiency apartment."

"That's me." Mercedes turned to her mother. "Will you be okay by yourself if I show him around the unit?"

"Yes. Go on ahead."

They left, and Carlita wandered to the front, peering anxiously out the window as she watched for the trolley and her family.

Had she inadvertently placed them in harm's way? She immediately dismissed the thought. The museum was open to the public. No one would suspect the nice little family. Not that she had asked them to do anything other than have a look around the museum and grounds and maybe even snap a few pictures.

She glanced at the wall clock for the umpteenth time. They had been gone a long time now, and Carlita had a bad feeling something had gone awry.

Chapter 18

Violet broke away from Shelby's grasp to admire a flowering bush. Her mother gently guided her back onto the sidewalk. "We'll visit the gardens in a little while."

"Can I pick a flower for Nana?"

"No. We mustn't pick the flowers." Shelby held her daughter's hand tightly as they climbed the steps and followed Tony onto *Darbylane Museum's* front porch.

The doorbell chimed, announcing their arrival.

Tony led his family to the counter. "Hello. We would like three tickets for a tour of the museum and gardens."

"Children twelve and under are free. Adults are ten dollars each."

He handed the employee a twenty. She held out three tickets. "This covers the cost of touring both the exhibits and grounds. Would you like a map?"

"No," Tony shook his head.

"Yes," Shelby said.

"I guess we would," Tony smiled.

The woman handed Shelby a map and Tony the tickets.

"Thank you." He waited until they entered the first exhibit area. "You need a map for us to find our way around? This place is small."

"Your mother will want to see the map," Shelby said.

"I'm surprised she didn't grab one the last time she was here."

"Probably because she told them she didn't need one," Shelby joked.

Violet skipped to the center of the room and a rectangular Plexiglas display case. "What's this?"

"It's a scale model of old Savannah," Tony said. "I think I see our building."

The trio leaned in.

"I see it, too." Shelby pointed to a replica of their building. "Violet, that's our house."

Violet pressed her nose against the side of the case. "We live there."

They circled the room and Shelby stopped occasionally to study the artwork. "I don't think I could come up with something this creative." She pointed to the piece, *Paralysis of Dreams*.

"What is it?" Tony peered at the painting, the silhouette of a man's side profile; his eyes squeezed shut and a look of pain on his face. Large bolts jutted out from both sides of his forehead. A dribble of blood ran from the corner of his mouth and down his chin. "That's disturbing."

"I have to agree, it's not my favorite."

They continued wandering through the exhibit, pausing occasionally to admire or comment on a piece of art.

"This is boooring," Violet whined.

"Stop, or we'll leave," her mother scolded. "You won't get to see the gardens."

Violet began to pout.

The trio picked up the pace and wandered through the next exhibit until they reached a sign with an arrow. *Gardens Tour.*

"Hurry." Violet darted down the steps and onto the paved path. She waited at the bottom for Tony and Shelby to catch up. "This is a magical garden."

"It's lovely." Shelby slowed to admire the flowers before they passed the herb garden. The herb garden abruptly ended when they reached a gravel path.

Violet broke free from her mother's grasp and ran ahead.

"Wait for us." Shelby ran after her and grabbed Violet's arm.

Tony caught up. "We need to stay together or you'll get lost."

"What's that?" Violet pointed to an arched arbor dotted with flowers. There was a white picket fence on each side of the arbor. Beyond the fence and lining the cobblestone path were pink and purple dahlias.

"Mommy. It's a princess cottage." Violet climbed the single step. Before Shelby could stop her, she grabbed a dangling roped cord and rang the brass bell attached to the doorpost.

"Violet Townsend Garlucci. Get back here!" Shelby scooped her daughter up. They made a quick retreat off the porch, but they weren't quite quick enough.

The door creaked open. An old man peered at them through the screen.

"I'm so sorry," Shelby apologized. "My daughter got away from me and rang your bell."

Violet wiggled out of her mother's arms. "This is a fairy cottage. A princess lives here."

The old man chuckled. "She does, does she?"

"Yes." Violet's head bobbed up and down. "Her name is fairy princess. She has a magic wand. She turns bad people into toads."

"And naughty little girls named Violet," Shelby said.

Tony joined them on the porch. "We're sorry to bother you."

"No worries. I was getting ready to check on the gardens." He joined them on the porch, the door slamming shut behind him.

"Henry." A woman's angry voice echoed out. "I told you to fix that door."

"I will Mabel. I'll get to it today," the man hollered back. The smile never left his face as he peered at Violet. "You look like a princess. In fact, I believe the name Violet means princess."

"It does?" Violet's eyes grew round as saucers. "When I grow up I'm going to live in a castle like Elsa and Anna."

"My name is Mr. Cagle. Would you like for me to show you the princesses' favorite flowers?"

Violet nodded.

He reached for Violet's hand, and his eyes met Shelby's eyes. "May I?"

Shelby smiled softly. "Yes."

The old man's wrinkled hand clasped Violet's small hand. They slowly made their way down the step while Shelby and Tony trailed behind.

Violet and Mr. Cagle stopped along the way to admire the blooming flowers. While they chatted, he told her the tale of the young princess who ran off from her parents, the king and queen, and became hopelessly lost in the gardens.

"I would never run off."

"Like you did a few minutes ago?" her mother asked.

"You must never run off again because princesses are very special. You don't want someone to take you away or for you to get lost." Mr. Cagle and Violet stopped when they reached the end of the cobblestone walkway and the white picket fence. "This is where I return home."

He reluctantly released his grip. Deep crinkles lined his kind gray eyes. He turned to Shelby and Tony. "Thank you for allowing me to share the magic of *Darbylane Gardens* with your daughter."

"Thank you for taking the time to show her." Shelby smiled warmly as their eyes met again, and she grabbed her daughter's hand. "Let's go have lunch in the café before we head home."

They began walking to the fence and gate. Violet slowed as she turned back to wave to Mr. Cagle. "He's the magic keeper of the gardens."

"I believe he is," Shelby agreed.

The trio passed the gardens again before circling back around. They stepped onto the patio leading to the museum's small café.

Once inside, they studied the limited menu before ordering two of the daily specials and a peanut butter and jelly sandwich for Violet.

During the meal, the young child chattered on about the enchanted garden, the fairy cottage and her princess status. They were finishing their lunch when Mr. Cagle appeared in the doorway.

His eyes scanned the room. When he spotted the family, he slowly shuffled over.

"Mr. Cagle." Tony placed his napkin on the table.

"I thought I heard you say you were having lunch here." He held out a small bouquet of bright flowers. "I picked these for Miss Violet."

"For me?" Violet slid out of her chair.

"These flowers are from the fairy garden. They're magical."

"Oh." Violet's mouth dropped open as she reached for the bouquet. "Magic flowers."

"Yes." The old man slowly nodded, his eyes twinkling with mischief. "When you get home, place them in a cup of water on the nightstand next to your bed. After you fall asleep tonight, the flowers will turn into fairies and sprinkle your room with magic fairy dust."

"Wow." Violet reverently grasped the bouquet with her pudgy hands.

"Now...you must be asleep for the fairies to appear."

"I will. I'll go to sleep right away."

"When the flowers die, it means it was time for the fairies to return home until they visit another princess, so you mustn't be sad."

"I won't," Violet solemnly promised. "I won't be sad."

"Thank you, Mr. Cagle," Tony said. "You made our afternoon here at the museum..."

"Enchanting," Shelby finished her husband's sentence.

"You're welcome. Violet reminds me of my great-granddaughter, Molly."

"Does she live nearby?"

"No. She lives in Atlanta. My wife and I will be moving there soon to be closer to her."

"And I'm sure she will love all of the wonderful stories you have to share," Shelby said. "She's one lucky little girl."

Mr. Cagle nodded. "Good-bye, Violet."

"Good-bye, Mr. Magical Man."

They all chuckled at Violet's nickname. After he left, Violet refused to release her grip on the bouquet of fairy flowers. She hung onto them tightly all the way home.

When they reached the apartment, Shelby and Violet went inside to place them in water while Tony returned to work.

He found his mother working alone. There were several shoppers inside, and Mercedes was nowhere in sight. "Where's Mercedes?"

"Interviewing a potential tenant," Carlita said. "I was beginning to worry about you. How did it go?"

"The museum was boring...definitely not my thing," Tony said. "The gardens were interesting. Violet made a new friend."

He told his mother how Violet ran off. "She rang the caretaker's bell."

"The caretaker...Mr. Cagle?" Carlita asked.

"Yes. He was a nice man. We apologized, and then he asked if he could show Violet the magical gardens. He's quite the storyteller, weaving tales of princesses and fairies."

"It sounds enchanting."

"Violet loved every minute of it. Before we left, he brought her a bouquet of magic flowers from the gardens."

"Magic flowers?"

"At night, the flowers turn into fairies and sprinkle the room with fairy dust," Tony chuckled. "Violet heard that and hasn't let go of those flowers."

"How adorable. Mr. Cagle sounds like a nice man. Did you meet Mrs. Cagle?"

"No, but we heard her. She was yelling at him from inside the cottage."

Carlita remembered the woman who stood glaring at Mercedes and her the previous night by the dumpster. "If it was the same woman Mercedes and I met, then I'm not surprised. You found nothing else?"

"No. Except for this." Tony handed his mother the map of the museum and gardens.

She glanced at the map. "Why didn't I get one of these the other day?"

"Shelby thought you might want it."

"I do. Tell her I said thank you."

The pawnshop phone began to ring.

"I'll let you get back to work," Carlita said. "Thank you for visiting the museum."

"I'm glad we went. We had fun," Tony said.

"Then we'll have to do it again soon...hold down the fort so you and your family can enjoy some time together." Carlita exited through the back of the pawnshop. The door to Tony's old efficiency was ajar. She could hear Mercedes chatting with the man they'd met earlier, so she headed home.

Upstairs, she grabbed her reading glasses and unfolded the map. At first, nothing caught her attention. She started to fold it back up when something caught her eye.

Chapter 19

The front door flew open. Mercedes waltzed into the apartment. "We found the perfect tenant," she sing-songed.

"The writer?"

"Yep. Angelica's rep, Gary, said she'll take the apartment. She's moving in next week." Mercedes waved a check in the air. "He wrote a check for an entire month's rent along with a security deposit."

"You're sure this famous writer will be a good fit?"

"She'll be perfect." Mercedes set the check and rental application on the desk.

"Take a look at this." Carlita handed her daughter the map.

"What is it?"

"It's the layout of the museum and grounds. Tony and Shelby picked it up during their visit today. I noticed something very interesting."

"A clue?" Mercedes held the map toward the light. "I see the museum and the parking lot. There's a caretaker's cottage in the far right-hand corner."

"And the alley where the dumpster is located is directly behind the caretaker's cottage," Carlita pointed out.

"Right."

"Look in the left-hand corner, directly across from the gardens and the cottage."

Mercedes squinted her eyes. "It looks like a cluster of storage buildings."

"I thought the same thing, although I don't remember seeing them the other night."

"Because we were too focused on following Astrid to see what she was up to," Mercedes said.

"Let's start with the theory that Astrid, a homeless person, was camping out in the storage buildings near the edge of the property. Someone at the museum discovered her and told her she had to leave."

"Which was around the same time Elvira spotted her digging through the dumpster, felt sorry for her and offered her a job."

"And a place to pitch her tent," Carlita added. "When someone who worked at the museum discovered Elvira had hired Astrid, they saw a perfect opportunity to slip her some cash in exchange for stealing the painting, or helping them make sure the painting left the property undetected."

"You think Astrid is an accomplice?" Mercedes carefully folded the map. "A museum employee would be familiar with the surveillance cameras, would possibly even be able to plan the ideal moment to steal the painting without getting caught."

"If they found a way to create a power outage *and* someone, in this case possibly Astrid, was covering their back," Carlita said. "My money is on Spelling, the curator. Astrid's been telling everyone how she's saving money to buy a plane ticket to Paris and that she's finally come up with the money because…"

"Because someone paid her," Mercedes finished her mother's sentence. "Which means she could be close to flying the coop. What if she has the painting? What if it's just Astrid?"

"It's possible," Carlita admitted. "Although I don't think she had the means to pull it off without an accomplice. Besides, I think it was planned ahead of time. This was in the works before Astrid appeared. She just happened to be in the right…or should I say wrong place at the wrong time."

"But how do we prove it?" Mercedes asked. "This is all merely speculation."

"There's something to Astrid's connection with the museum and the fact she doesn't let her backpack out of her sight. We know she's going back to the museum. She told Elvira today is her last day in Savannah and she had something to take care of. She's packing up and heading out tomorrow. That means if something is going to happen, it's going to happen today."

"So you want to follow Astrid again to try to figure out who else may be behind the theft."

"I do. If Astrid is involved, I believe she's going to make contact with her connection one last time," Carlita said. "Tonight will be her last chance."

Beep. Beep. Beep. The outer doorbell chimed. Carlita popped out of the chair and hurried to the living room window. "It's Elvira."

The doorbell began beeping again, this time nonstop. "Hold your horses," Carlita hollered as she ran down the steps. "Give me time to get to the door." She flung the door open.

"We don't have time. Follow me." Elvira didn't wait for Carlita to reply and marched down the alley.

Carlita hurried to keep up. "Where's the fire?"

"You'll see."

The women reached the parking area, walking between the vehicles until they reached Astrid's tent.

"I was on my way out to run some errands. Something told me to take a quick look inside Astrid's tent." Elvira unzipped the tent door. "I always go with my gut. It never steers me wrong." She reached inside and pulled out a dingy gray backpack.

"Astrid's backpack," Carlita said breathlessly. "She left it behind."

"She was running late for her job this morning and must've forgotten it."

"Did you look inside?"

"Not yet. I figured I owed you one, what with everything I put you through lately."

"You mean always," Carlita said.

"Do you want to criticize me or do you want to see what's inside?"

"I want to see what's inside."

Elvira shoved her hand in the small front pocket. "Empty."

She unzipped the next section and pulled out a hairbrush. She set it on the welcome mat and reached inside again. There was a Ziploc bag containing a travel size tube of toothpaste and a toothbrush. "That's all for this section. Let's try the next one."

Elvira balanced the bag on the mat as she unzipped the main compartment. She reached inside and pulled out a plastic grocery bag. Crammed inside the bag were two pairs of shorts, two faded t-shirts, three pair of threadbare underwear and a cheap pair of dime store flip-flops.

"Poor thing," Carlita's throat clogged as she gazed at the woman's meager belongings.

"At least she doesn't have to pay checked bag fees on the plane. There's something else in here." Elvira gingerly pulled out a small, rectangular wrapped box. "It's a present."

"We should open it."

"No way." Elvira snatched it back. "This is a gift."

Carlita ran a light hand over the top. "It's hard. Maybe she bought you a thank-you gift which is why she didn't want you peeking inside her backpack."

"You're right, which means we don't open it." Elvira eased the wrapped package back inside.

"C'mon. If you can't bring yourself to open it, I will."

"Fine." Elvira pulled a small pocketknife from her pants pocket and flicked it open. "I'll open one end. That's it." She ran the blade of the small knife under the strip of tape and pried it off. "Ha!"

"What is it?" Carlita leaned forward, eager to catch a glimpse of the contents.

Elvira turned it so she could see. "It's a telescope. Astrid must've read my mind. I've always wanted one for stargazing."

"Or spying on your neighbors," Carlita muttered. "Fine. She's giving you a telescope as a parting gift, which explains why she didn't want you snooping around her stuff."

"She probably dug it out of a dumpster." Elvira carefully folded the wrapping paper and pressed on the piece of tape. "The end of the box is a little beat up. It's the thought that counts."

She returned the bag of clothes before zipping the backpack and setting it in the tent. "This entire time we thought she was hiding something and all she was doing was hiding a surprise gift." Elvira turned accusing eyes on Carlita. "Do you always have to believe the worst about people?"

"Me?" Carlita could feel her face grow warm. "Elvira Cobb, you are the most trying person I have ever met. You do one kind thing for a person, and now you think you're a saint."

"I didn't say I was a saint, but you've been suspicious of poor Astrid from the moment you met her."

"*You're* the one who told me she's using a fake name."

"People lie all of the time. It doesn't make them a criminal," Elvira argued.

"But it usually means they have something to hide."

"Well, I hope this settles your suspicion of Astrid. Besides, after tomorrow, she'll be long gone."

"And we're still under suspicion for the painting's theft," Carlita pointed out. "We're back to square one."

"I've got some leads I'm working on. I think I might have a break in the case soon."

Carlita followed Elvira to the alley. "What kinds of leads?"

"Uh-uh. I'm sorry, Carlita. I'm working alone from here on out."

"Don't you want me to help clear my name?"

"No. It's just that..." Elvira's voice trailed off.

"What?"

"You kind of screwed up on the intel mission by getting caught on camera inside the museum's storage area. I can't take that chance again. I've decided it's best for you to leave this one to the experts."

"You," Carlita guessed.

"Yes."

"Oh, brother." Carlita threw her hands up in the air. "Suit yourself. I hope you are able to figure out what happened to the painting."

"Oh, I will. Mark my words." Elvira slipped back inside her apartment and closed the door behind her.

Mercedes stood in the doorway waiting for her mother. "What was that all about?"

"Astrid left her backpack behind, so Elvira searched it."

"And?"

"Other than some meager personal belongings which nearly broke my heart, there was a wrapped gift. Elvira is convinced it's a thank-you gift for her, which is why Astrid didn't want her touching the backpack."

"So now what?"

"She's working on some other leads and basically told me to butt out," Carlita said.

"Butt out?"

"She claims I messed up and wants me to leave the investigation to the experts, namely her."

"You don't want to follow Astrid again tonight, to see what she's up to?"

Carlita gazed at her daughter thoughtfully. Despite the fact that Astrid had a legitimate reason for guarding her backpack, something still wasn't sitting right. "No. I do. We're missing something. Elvira mentioned Astrid was packing up and leaving first thing tomorrow morning, but she had to take care of something first. She's working now, so if she's taking care of something, she's doing it after she finishes her security job at the festival."

"I say we take in the festival later this afternoon before it shuts down. We hang around after it ends and then follow Astrid," Mercedes said. "If she told Elvira she had something to take care of, I'm guessing she'll want to do it after she finishes working."

"And before tomorrow morning."

*****

The afternoon passed slowly. Carlita spent most of it mulling over the suspects and Elvira's comment about how she was following up on something. Were the authorities close to making an arrest?

If Elvira knew Astrid was lying about her identity yet still trusted the woman enough to hire her, perhaps there were others in Elvira's employ who shouldn't be trusted. She thought about Dernice and her past criminal record.

Carlita returned to the theory someone on the inside knew about Dernice's background, despite leaving the information off the application, and that was the reason *EC Security Services* was awarded the job...as a setup.

The women ate a late lunch, and Mercedes helped her mother clear the table. "Hey, Rambo. Would you like to go for a walk?"

Carlita placed their leftovers in the fridge. "You want me to tag along?"

"Nah." Mercedes reached for Rambo's leash. "I was thinking maybe I would stop by Sam's place to see if Sadie wanted to go with us."

Carlita lifted a brow. "And maybe even Sam?"

"Maybe." Mercedes frowned. "Don't look at me like that."

"Like what?"

"Like you're trying to marry me off to Sam or something."

"Marriage is a bit premature," her mother teased. "But I think it's wonderful you and Sam have made amends and are finally friends. Perhaps even something more someday."

"Yeah, well you might be sorely disappointed." Mercedes reached for the door handle.

"Might be," Carlita said. "I like the sounds of that."

Mercedes didn't reply as she coaxed Rambo into the hall.

Carlita hurried to the living room window facing the alley.

Mercedes and Rambo emerged first. Sadie trotted onto the stoop. Her daughter turned back, a goofy smile on her face. Sam joined her and Carlita's heart melted.

"Will you look at that?" Carlita whispered. "Miracles never cease." She watched them stroll to the end of the alley and turn right, toward the trolley stop and the street that led to *Morrell Park*.

She turned to go when she noticed movement near the side of Elvira's building. Her neighbor scurried into the alley, furtively glancing over her shoulder. Instead of stopping at her backdoor, she hustled to the parking area.

Carlita eased her door open and stepped onto the balcony.

Elvira had reached the corner. She glanced over her shoulder again, this time misjudging her steps. She tripped on the corner of a gutter that was jutting out. Her arms flailed wildly as she attempted to regain her balance.

"Now what is she up to?"

Elvira regained her footing before disappearing around the side of the building.

Carlita stepped back inside and settled in at her desk where she began balancing the business accounts. Despite the seasonal slowdown, *Savannah Swag* was still turning a decent profit. Now that the apartments were filled, they would have some extra money to help keep *Ravello's* afloat.

Carlita scrutinized the restaurant's food costs and wondered if she should get quotes from other purveyors. She jotted a note to ask Pete which company or companies he used for *Parrot House Restaurant* and then clicked out of the screen.

Mercedes burst through the door. "Oh my gosh. Ma...did you see what's going on next door at Elvira's place?"

Chapter 20

"No." Carlita turned. "Now what?"

"Check it out." Mercedes darted to the window, and Carlita joined her. A police car was parked next to Elvira's back door.

"I hope they're not coming back here again."

"I don't think so. I saw the cops go inside Elvira's place. There are two of them."

"Hard telling what that woman has managed to get herself into this time."

Another few minutes passed before the door opened. Detective Polivich stepped into the alley. Elvira was next, followed by a uniformed officer.

Polivich opened the back door to the patrol car.

Elvira shook her head.

"I wish I could hear what they're saying," Mercedes said in a low voice.

"Me, too."

The detective turned to Elvira, a stern expression on his face.

Elvira shook her head again as she said something.

The detective grasped her arm and guided her into the back of the patrol car.

"Uh-oh. They're taking her down to the station." Carlita pressed her forehead against the windowpane. "Can you tell if she's handcuffed?"

"No. It doesn't look like it."

The women stood motionless as they watched the detective and the officer climb into the front of the car. The vehicle slowly made its way down the alley and disappeared from sight. "Glenda Fox said the authorities were close to making an arrest."

"They must have something on her," Mercedes said.

Dernice stepped into the alley. Carlita hurried onto the balcony. "Hey! Dernice."

Elvira's sister shaded her eyes as she looked up. "Yeah?"

"What happened?"

"With what?"

"With Elvira. She left with the police."

"Eh," Dernice crossed the alley. "It's a minor misunderstanding. Elvira salvaged a picture frame from the museum's recycle bin and brought it home. It still had a museum sticker on the back. When the cops searched our place the other day, they found it. Elvira told them she pulled it out of the junk pile. I guess they didn't believe her because they took it as evidence and now the museum's curator is claiming it was stolen."

"You're kidding."

"Nope." Dernice shook her head. "I think they plan to pin the painting theft on Elvira."

"Are you going to try to bail her out?" Mercedes leaned both elbows on the railing.

"Nah. We finally hired an attorney." Dernice waved dismissively. "He's on his way down to the police station now. Ten bucks says she's back by dinnertime. I gotta get going."

Carlita waved good-bye and followed Mercedes inside. "I don't think Elvira is going to have as easy of a time as Dernice seems to think she will."

"Me, either," Mercedes agreed. "Are we still on for a trip to the festival later?"

"Yeah. I think Astrid is up to something."

"I was gonna say, even if we don't keep an eye on Astrid, you might want to check it out." Mercedes told her mother she found out from Sam that *LaFitte Square* was hosting a food truck festival.

"Food truck festival?" Carlita's interest was piqued. "You know what? We need to get in on these food festivals, or the haunted restaurant tour business." She warmed to the idea. "Mercedes, this is brilliant. I can't wait to check it out."

It was nearly five by the time Carlita and her daughter headed to *LaFitte Square's* festival. Food trucks, parked bumper to bumper, lined the square. The tantalizing aroma of fried foods encompassed the center.

"Where should we start?"

"Eating or searching for Astrid?" Carlita joked.

"Either one." Mercedes motioned to one of the food trucks. "I see an Italian food truck. They stepped over to the *Pasta Paradise* food truck, and Carlita perused the menu:

Pasta and Meatballs

Custom Flatbread Pizza

Eleven Layer Lasagna

Manicotti

Rigatoni

Italian Sampler: Mozzarella Cheese Sticks, Eleven Layer Lasagna and Meatballs

Freshly Baked Bread

Mama Mia's Italian Ice

"You got any cash on you?" Carlita nudged her daughter.

"I do." Mercedes pulled her cell phone and a twenty-dollar bill from her pocket. "What should we try?"

"The Italian Sampler." Carlita ordered one sampler, extra marinara sauce and two Italian Ices.

"That'll be nineteen dollars and ten cents."

Carlita handed him the twenty. "Keep the change." She carried the tray to a nearby picnic table. "There isn't a lot of food here for almost twenty bucks." She sliced a small piece of the lasagna. "Not bad. It's a little dry and needs more sauce."

Mercedes took a bite. "Yep."

They sampled each of the items; both agreeing the food was tasty considering it was prepared in such a cramped space.

"You really think we should try a food truck?"

"Sure. Why not," Mercedes said. "I bet we could lease a truck for a coupla months, to see how it goes. We gotta get *Ravello's* on the map."

They finished the food and tossed the wrappers in the trash before making their rounds. All the while, Carlita kept an eye out for Astrid. She finally spotted her standing near a park bench talking to a young couple.

Carlita took a quick step back to move out of her line of vision, but it was too late. Astrid spotted them and gave a small wave.

"We had better say hello."

Astrid met them near the center of the square. "Hello, Mrs. Garlucci."

"Hello, Astrid. Have you met my daughter, Mercedes?"

"Hi." Mercedes smiled.

"Hey. Are you here to check out the competition?" Astrid asked.

"You could say that. Elvira said you'll be leaving soon."

"I am." Astrid nodded. "I'm leaving first thing tomorrow morning."

"I hope you have a safe trip. Perhaps we'll see you again sometime if you ever fly back to the States."

"Maybe."

The trio made small talk for a few more minutes, and then Astrid excused herself.

Mercedes watched her walk away. "She doesn't strike me as the criminal type. Why do you think she's hiding her true identity?"

"I don't know." Carlita gazed at her thoughtfully. "She doesn't strike me as a thief, either, but she is lying. Why is she leaving the country? Why was she living on the streets, scrounging through dumpsters for food?"

"Drugs?" Mercedes guessed. "Maybe she has a drug problem."

"I suppose." The women wandered around the area until the food trucks began closing up shop and pulling out of the square.

"We need to find somewhere to hang out where Astrid doesn't see us," Mercedes said. "We could go to the next square where we still have a visual. That way, we can see which direction Astrid heads."

"I agree."

The women strolled to the next square, this one partially concealed by manicured bushes and shrubs.

"This is a good hiding spot." Carlita squinted her eyes. "Maybe a little too good. I can't see *LaFitte Square.*"

"I got it covered. I figured we might need a few supplies." Mercedes shrugged off her backpack and set it on the ground. She unzipped the main compartment, reached inside and pulled out a pair of binoculars.

"Why didn't I think of that?" Carlita asked.

"Because I did." Mercedes handed them to her mother.

"What else do you have in there?"

"A flashlight, a multi-tool and this." Mercedes brandished her handgun.

"Mercedes. Put that thing away!" Carlita's eyes darted around the square.

"You asked."

"Why on earth did you bring a gun?"

"I always carry it. That's why I got a WCL - a weapon carry license. I think you oughta get one, too."

"I don't want to carry a gun around." Carlita held the binoculars to her eyes and adjusted the focus wheel. "The trucks are gone." She shifted the binoculars and scanned the square. "There...I see Astrid."

Mercedes consulted her watch. "It's six-twenty. She'll be heading out soon."

"Your turn." Carlita handed her daughter the binoculars and eased onto the bench. Several pedestrians strolled past. A couple slowed, giving Carlita and her daughter a strange look.

"We're birdwatching," Carlita joked.

"Huh." The couple kept going. The woman turned back once before whispering something in the man's ear.

"I have a visual. Astrid is on the move." Mercedes shoved the binoculars in the backpack, zipped it shut and slung it over her shoulder. "Stay low. She's heading this way." She sank down onto the bench and shrank back as Astrid passed by. She was moving at a fast clip.

"We gotta go." The women hopped off the bench and jogged across the square. They stepped onto the sidewalk and began following Astrid. "You know where she's going," Carlita said breathlessly.

"The museum?"

"Yes, at least that's the direction she's headed." Carlita was certain Astrid was returning to the museum until she changed directions and began heading toward *Walton Square*.

"She's going back toward the apartment," Mercedes said.

"Yes." Carlita held out her hand. "I think you're right. She's heading home. We might as well take our time."

The women slowed their pace, and Astrid quickly disappeared from sight.

"This surveillance operation was a bust." Mercedes shifted her gaze. "The museum is right around the corner. We might as well go check it out since we walked all the way over here. Maybe something will stand out as a clue."

"I suppose."

The women circled the block and approached the front entrance to *Darbylane Museum*. "It's closed." Mercedes pointed to the sign affixed to the front of the locked entrance gate. "They close at six."

"We just missed it."

They walked around the side to the corner where the storage sheds were located. "This is where I think Astrid was staying until Elvira offered to let her camp out in her yard," Carlita said.

"And the caretaker's cottage is back here?" Mercedes asked. "Sam and I ran into Violet and Shelby during our walk. Violet told me all about the magical cottage, the flowers and the fairies who come out at night. The caretaker has convinced Violet that she's a princess."

"I heard." Carlita grinned, and then changed the subject. "According to the map Tony gave me, the cottage is in the opposite corner, over here."

The women wandered to the other end of the property. Through the bars, Carlita spotted a section of white picket fence. Brightly colored flowers lined the cobblestone walkway.

"I see a porch." Mercedes pointed through the bars. "It does look enchanting, almost magical."

"It's lovely, just what a magical cottage should be."

The women were still admiring the cottage when the front door opened. An elderly man crept onto the porch. A woman, the same one who noticed them near the dumpster the previous night, joined him.

Mercedes pressed a finger to her lips, as they inched off to the side.

"She's not going to show," the woman said. "I told you we never should've trusted her."

"Relax Mabel. She'll be here. She said she would and she will."

"She had better."

There was a moment of silence. "You don't think that stupid woman from the security company got her hands on it first, do you?"

"Elvira Cobb?" The old man cackled. "She's not bright enough to put two and two together."

"Don't be so sure. What time is it?"

The man looked at his watch. "It's almost seven. She said she would be here at seven."

Carlita glanced around. They needed to hide, to see who showed up.

Mercedes was a step ahead of her mother. She grabbed her hand and dragged her behind a row of metal trashcans.

Carlita hit her knees, and a sharp pain shot down her leg. She bit her lip to prevent herself from crying out.

The duo remained motionless for several minutes, until Carlita's foot went numb. She shifted slightly, to relieve the numbness when Mercedes stopped her. She jabbed a finger in the direction of the museum.

Carlita's heart skipped a beat as a familiar figure approached.

Chapter 21

Astrid strolled to the back of the property and called out.

Carlita and Mercedes watched as the elderly man approached the wrought iron gate. He said something to Astrid before opening the gate and motioning for her to step inside. Moments later, they disappeared from sight.

Mercedes bolted from their hiding spot and hurried to the corner of the property.

Carlita wiggled her toes until the numbness subsided and then limped across the alley to join her daughter. She could hear voices coming from the direction of the cottage's porch but couldn't make out what was being said.

"Look." Mercedes nudged her mother. "She has the backpack."

Sure enough, Astrid was carrying her backpack. She eased it off her shoulder and unzipped it before reaching inside. She pulled out the wrapped package Carlita and Elvira found earlier and handed it to the woman.

"What..." Carlita's mind whirled.

"What is that?" Mercedes whispered under her breath. "A present?"

"Yes. It's a tabletop telescope. Elvira thought it was a gift for her, but it appears it's a gift for the caretaker and his wife."

The woman took the gift and carefully set it on the wicker chair next to the front door before embracing Astrid. The man hugged her next. They stood talking for several long moments.

They stepped off the porch, now close enough for Mercedes and Carlita to eavesdrop. "You're staying with the lady who owns the security company tonight?" the man asked.

"Yes. I'm leaving in the morning." They made small talk, and finally, Astrid turned on her heel and began walking away.

Mother and daughter dove for cover, making it behind the trashcans without a second to spare as Astrid moseyed through the gate.

The man's steps were slow as he leaned heavily on his cane and followed Astrid out. "...and call us dear, when you finally make it to wherever you're going."

"Thank you, Mr. Cagle. I hope you enjoy your special birthday gift."

"I'm sure I will." The man waved a final time. He watched Astrid walk away before closing the gate behind him.

Cagle picked up his cane, straightened his back and with quick steps made his way back toward the porch.

"The old man made a miraculous recovery," Mercedes whispered sarcastically. "Astrid gave them a gift."

"No." Carlita's heart skipped a beat as the pieces began falling into place. "I don't think that's a present. I think it's the missing artwork."

"Disguised as a gift - a small telescope?"

"Yep. Not only was Elvira set up, but also Astrid. For some reason, the caretakers had her thinking she was holding onto a birthday gift for the man. They tricked her. They gave Astrid the painting to hang onto."

"You don't think she knows what it is?"

"I...I don't know what to think. Judging by the comment she made to Mr. Cagle, I don't think so. Detective Polivich needs to get over here to take a closer look at what Astrid just handed over to the caretakers."

Mercedes pulled her cell phone from her pocket. "I don't have his number. I'll call the main number for the Savannah Police Department."

It took several tries and transfers before Mercedes finally reached the detective.

"Detective Polivich speaking."

"Detective Polivich. This is Mercedes Garlucci." Mercedes paused.

"Yes. Carlita Garlucci is my mother. We think we may have important information and possibly a lead in the whereabouts of the missing artwork." Mercedes covered the phone. "What is the closest square?"

"I don't know, but *Savannah Dry Cleaners* is around the corner," Carlita said.

"Can you meet me at *Savannah Dry Cleaners* downtown? It's not far from the museum."

"An hour?" Mercedes frowned. "It may be too late by then."

"Fine. We'll see you in ten." She disconnected the call. "He's on his way."

The women stayed close to the building as they retraced their steps and made their way to the dry cleaners around the corner.

Carlita cast an anxious glance in the direction of the museum. "This all makes perfect sense. Astrid is an innocent accomplice. The caretaker and his wife stole the painting. They met Astrid when she was hanging around here. They played her. They pretended to care for her all the while using her to conceal the painting."

The detective pulled up in an unmarked car a short time later. "This better be good."

"Are you still detaining Elvira?" Carlita asked.

"Yes. That woman is one of the most aggravating people I have ever met."

Carlita snorted. "It took you all this time to figure that out?"

"What's the big emergency?"

Mercedes briefly outlined what she and her mother had observed and overheard.

"You think the security company employee, Astrid Herve, was inadvertently hanging onto the stolen artwork for the museum's caretakers?"

"Disguised as a birthday gift for the caretaker, Mr. Cagle," Carlita added.

"You're sure?"

"No. I mean, we watched Astrid hand the wrapped gift to Mrs. Cagle. She told Mr. Cagle she hoped he enjoyed his surprise gift and then thanked him and his wife for befriending her."

"And you're sure the woman, Astrid, has no idea what's inside?"

"Not from the conversation we overheard. We believe the Cagles tricked her into holding onto it for them. As of half an hour ago, they still had possession of the package." Carlita almost mentioned the telescope, but revealing what she knew would only raise more questions about her involvement. She decided it was best for the investigators to discover what was inside the wrapped package on their own.

The detective returned to his car to call for backup. Two more unmarked vehicles arrived on scene moments later, and he briefly explained the situation. "Let's go check it out."

Carlita and Mercedes started to follow. Polivich stopped them. "You're safer staying here."

"You wouldn't be here if it wasn't for us," Mercedes said.

"I could arrest you for interfering in a police investigation."

"You wouldn't dare," Mercedes gasped. "We're only trying to help."

"We'll stay back," Carlita promised. "I think it's only fair we're allowed to see if we were right."

The detective eyed them silently before relenting. "Fine. But stay out of the way."

Carlita assured them they would stay far away, but close enough to watch the events unfold.

The authorities blocked off the alley and the street. Carlita and Mercedes made their way to the back of one of the police vehicles. They watched as several officers, along with Detective Polivich, entered the property.

"What if we were way off?" Mercedes whispered.

The officers were gone a long time, and Carlita was beginning to wonder if they had it all wrong. "It's possible," she admitted.

Finally, the detective reappeared. He and a uniformed officer escorted the elderly couple from the property to the back of a patrol car and placed them inside.

A four-door sedan arrived and parked behind one of the patrol cars. Gaston Spelling sprang from the vehicle and hurried to the back of the museum.

Detective Polivich met him near the gate. There was a brief conversation, and then they disappeared from sight.

"Let's go." Mercedes grabbed her mother's hand and dragged her to the gate. They approached the caretaker's cottage where a cluster of officers gathered. Polivich and the museum's curator stood off to the side.

Carlita hurried to join them. "You found it."

Polivich turned to face her, his stern expression softening. "As a matter of fact, we did. The Cagles were in possession of the stolen artwork. Now, all we have to do is figure out if there are additional accomplices."

"Meaning Astrid Herve," Carlita said.

"Yes. We'll know more as soon as we have a chance to question the Cagles."

Chapter 22

"Astrid is officially off the hook." Carlita breezed into the apartment.

"She really didn't know what was inside the wrapped package?" Mercedes joined her mother in the living room.

"No. The Cagles confessed. They told the investigators they tricked Astrid under the premise Mrs. Cagle was surprising her husband. She asked Astrid to hang onto his birthday present."

"What about the museum's curator, Mr. Spelling?" Mercedes asked. "We saw him hand Astrid something."

"It was money. Gaston Spelling was sympathetic to Astrid's predicament," Carlita said. "She was hiding out in the sheds on the edge of the property. Spelling spotted her one evening on his way out and asked her to leave. When he found out she was homeless, he felt sorry for her and started giving her money."

"Surely, there are homeless shelters in the area," Mercedes said.

"Yes, but Astrid refused to go because of her phobia of enclosed spaces," her mother reminded her. "And the women's shelter was full."

"Where do the caretakers...the Cagles come in?"

"According to Astrid, the couple befriended her, even inviting her to the cottage for dinner."

Carlita told her daughter that early the previous week, after Elvira's interview at the museum for the security job, she found Astrid digging in the dumpster and offered her a temporary job, working under the table. "The couple knew she was working with Elvira."

"It must've taken some planning to pull off the theft," Mercedes said.

"Yes. The Cagles tripped the power source, knowing the alarm would go down until it kicked into backup mode."

"What about the surveillance cameras? I'm sure the cameras were on battery backup."

"They were." Carlita nodded. "Except that someone had removed the backup batteries."

"The Cagles."

"Mr. Cagle shut down the power, knew he had a couple of minutes before the alarm reset and knew the cameras were off. He sneaked into the museum, grabbed the painting and took off before the alarm came back up. The couple knew the authorities would search the premises and they needed to get the painting out of there."

"This is where Astrid comes in," Mercedes guessed.

"The painting was already protected inside a special Plexiglas shadowbox, both waterproof and humidity controlled. They placed the special box and painting inside the telescope box. It was small...small enough to conceal. Mrs. Cagle tracked Astrid down and told her she had a very special gift for Mr. Cagle, a birthday present, and she didn't want him to find it. She asked Astrid to hang onto it for her. Astrid agreed."

"But what if Astrid got caught with the painting or Elvira started snooping around Astrid's things?"

"I guess it was a risk they were willing to take. The Cagles were never suspects, having lived in the caretaker's cottage and caring for the grounds for years."

"But why would the couple steal the painting? Why now?"

"I wondered the same thing. Detective Polivich said they were angry and bitter. The museum's board had decided it was time for the Cagles to retire and move out of the caretaker's cottage. They thought they would be living there forever. They came up with a plan to help themselves to a 'parting gift.'"

"Some parting gift," Mercedes rolled her eyes. "Elvira should thank you for saving her hide, not to mention her company's reputation."

"I'm not holding my breath," Carlita said.

"What happened to Astrid?"

"The authorities are trying to get Astrid's plane ticket changed without incurring change fees. Elvira offered to let her hang around for a couple more days until they get it straightened out."

"In her tent?"

"Yes. I don't know how that poor woman is going to manage on an overseas plane ride if she's claustrophobic."

"So Elvira is off the hook, too?"

"As far as I know. There was some sort of mix-up over the discarded painting frames. One of the employees had placed several empty frames in the recycle pile by accident," Carlita said. "Elvira saw them and decided to bring one of them home."

The downstairs bell rang.

"That's probably Elvira." Carlita hurried down the steps.

Astrid stood on the stoop. "I'm sorry to bother you, Mrs. Garlucci. I wanted to stop by to thank you for everything."

"You're welcome. I'm sorry the Cagles weren't the people you thought they were. You're leaving tomorrow."

"Yes, ma'am."

"Why don't you come in?" Carlita motioned her inside.

"I-I don't want to bother you."

"It's no bother. I insist." Carlita led Astrid up the steps and into the apartment. She motioned to her backpack. "You're taking your backpack with you?"

"Yes."

"Now that the painting is off your hands, you have some extra room in your backpack for clothes."

338

Carlita eyed her critically. "I think you and Mercedes might be close to the same size."

Astrid shifted her backpack. "You don't have to give me anything."

Mercedes joined them. "Ma's right. I have a closetful of clothes I rarely wear. Let's go see what we can find."

Mercedes and Astrid headed to Mercedes' bedroom to dig through the closet while Carlita fixed sandwiches for lunch. As she worked, she thought about how lonely Astrid must be. She wondered what would possess a woman to just up and leave the country with barely more than the clothes on her back.

She finished grilling the chicken parmesan paninis and wandered into Mercedes' bedroom. "I made a quick lunch. Would you like to join us?"

Astrid hesitated.

"I insist."

"Ma makes the best paninis."

The women joined Carlita while she placed the plates of food on the dining room table. "Would you like tea or a Coke?"

"Water will be fine." Astrid stared at the food hungrily. "You didn't have to make me lunch. First, you give me clothes, not to mention helping to clear my name and now this. It's too much."

"It was no trouble." Carlita poured three glasses of ice water. Mercedes helped her mother carry that, along with napkins and a container of pasta salad to the table.

"Merci." Astrid reached for her glass of water.

Carlita took the seat across from the young woman. "Are you ready for the long flight tomorrow?"

"I hope so. I haven't been on a plane in years. I went to France, years ago when I was younger."

"Before you became claustrophobic," Carlita reached for the dish of pasta. "I hope you don't have trouble on the plane. It will be a very long flight."

Astrid tugged on a chunk of melted cheese. "I have a confession. I'm not claustrophobic."

Carlita and Mercedes exchanged a quick glance. "You're not?"

"No." Astrid set the sandwich down and pushed the plate away. "I'm sorry."

"For what?"

"For lying. For lying to you. For lying to Elvira...for not trusting the people who were trying to help me," Astrid said. "I...it's just that I didn't know who to trust."

"So you're not claustrophobic," Carlita said.

"And I'm not Astrid Herve. I made that name up." Astrid hung her head.

"We know," Carlita said softly. "Elvira told us Astrid wasn't your real name."

Astrid's head shot up. "Elvira knows?"

"Of course. She runs a security and investigative company. She checked you out before she hired you."

Astrid's jaw dropped. "And she hired me knowing I was lying?"

"Yes," Carlita nodded. "And she let you stay on her property."

Sudden tears welled up in Astrid's eyes. Her lower lip started to tremble. "Why?"

"I suspect she knew there was more to your story. To her credit, she trusted you more than I did."

"You shouldn't have trusted me," Astrid said.

"Why?" Carlita asked. "Other than the obvious reasons. My guess is you're hiding from something...or someone."

Astrid nervously sipped her water. Carlita could see the internal turmoil raging inside the woman. "Someone."

"Someone who wishes you harm?"

"It's my ex-boyfriend. My real name is Valerie Maxim. I'm from Charleston, South Carolina. He held me hostage. He was going to kill me. I escaped with the clothes on my back, my driver's license and passport. I fled here to Savannah to stay with a friend. My cousin warned me Damian was planning to come down here. I couldn't risk putting my friend in danger, so I left. I didn't dare use my cell phone or my credit cards figuring he would track me down."

"So you were living on the streets," Mercedes said. "What about going to a women's shelter?"

"I tried. They were all full." Astrid clasped her hands. "When Elvira offered me a job paying cash, I knew I had a chance...a chance to go so far away that Damian would never find me, never follow me."

"This is awful. Don't you have family who can take you in?" Carlita asked. "What about the authorities in Charleston? You should stay and fight. You could get a restraining order."

"I have no family. Damian's family...they're very powerful people. No one would believe me. I can't go back there." A tear trickled down Astrid's cheek. She quickly swiped at it. "I have an old friend who lives in Paris. If I can make it to Paris, I have a place to stay until I can get on my feet."

"Are you sure you want to do this?" Carlita asked gently.

"It's either that or always be looking over my shoulder waiting for Damian to find me. You don't know him. You don't know what he's capable of."

"I'm sorry, Astrid." Carlita didn't know what else to say. She couldn't imagine feeling she had no choice but to flee the country.

Astrid stared at the plate of food.

"You should try to eat something."

"At least you have somewhere to go," Mercedes said. "You had enough money for the plane ticket?"

"Plus a couple hundred extra bucks."

"I do have one question. It's been bothering me since I found out about the package you thought was a gift that you were holding onto for Mrs. Cagle," Carlita said.

"You're wondering why I agreed to hang onto it," Astrid guessed.

"Yes. Especially after finding out a valuable piece of artwork had been stolen from the museum."

"They were such a nice old couple, always inviting me to dinner. Never in a million years would I have suspected they were involved in the theft. Mrs. Cagle asked me to do one small favor. She seemed so excited about surprising her husband."

"Did she tell you what the gift was?" Carlita asked.

"No. She made me promise not to tell anyone. She said it was a surprise."

"It certainly was." Carlita shoved her chair away from the table. "I'll be right back."

She strolled out of the apartment, to the pawnshop and the cash register. Carlita swiped her access card and opened the cash drawer.

Tony strode to the back. "Whatcha doin', Ma?"

"I need money. Cash." She counted out four hundred and sixty-two dollars. Carlita pocketed the larger bills and left the smaller ones in the drawer.

"Why do you need cash?"

"I'm giving some money to Astrid. Write an IOU. Take it out of my next paycheck or mark it as a charitable contribution. I'll explain later."

She left her son, a puzzled expression on his face, and returned to the apartment. "This is for you." Carlita placed the money on the table next to Astrid.

Astrid began shaking her head. "I can't take this. I can't accept your money. You've been so generous. You got me out of trouble. You gave me clothes and food. I can't accept your money."

"I insist."

Astrid stared at the money, tears freely streaming down her cheeks.

"It's only four hundred dollars, but this will buy you food, public transportation and give you a little breathing room."

Mercedes, who had been quietly watching, left the table. She returned with more money. "I have some cash, too. I won't need it anytime soon." She placed a small stack of bills on top of the pile.

Astrid coughed and then burst into tears, long wracking sobs shaking her body.

Carlita wrapped her arms around the woman, her heart breaking at the anguish she must be feeling. "It's gonna be all right. Just think. This is a new beginning for you, Astrid."

Astrid nodded as she continued to cry uncontrollably. "I hope so."

Carlita held tight until the sobbing subsided.

Astrid sniffled loudly. "I'm sorry. I didn't mean to come unglued."

"It's okay. We all need a good cry once in a while." Carlita straightened her back. "Now. Take the money. If you ever return to Savannah, promise me you'll stop by to let us know how you're doing."

"I will." Astrid reached for the money. "I didn't tell you to make you feel sorry for me."

"You didn't have to. I already knew you were in a bad place," Carlita pointed to the sandwich. "Now eat your lunch."

The conversation turned to Astrid's plans once she arrived in Paris, and Carlita was relieved to discover she had given some serious thought to her future.

Carlita offered to let her sleep on the sofa for the night, but Astrid politely declined. She told them she would be leaving early the next morning. "Elvira is dropping me off at the airport. I'm not very good at good-byes."

"I'm not either." Carlita and Mercedes walked her to the alley. Both gave her a warm hug.

"Au revoir," Astrid whispered. "Until we meet again."

"Until we meet again," Carlita echoed.

Chapter 23

Astrid returned to her tent while Mercedes and her mother returned home.

"I feel sorry for Astrid," Mercedes said.

"Me, too. And I feel guilty," Carlita confessed. "I thought I had it all figured out. I was almost convinced it was just Astrid, not the sweet old couple, the Cagles. We always expect the worst of some people, judging before we know all of the facts and accepting based on what we see or hear. This is a lesson to me, that I should get all of my facts straight before passing judgment."

Carlita's mood was somber the rest of the evening as she thought about Astrid's heartbreaking circumstances.

Mercedes was quiet, too, and a lingering sadness stayed with both of them.

Before heading to bed, Carlita stepped out on the balcony, her eyes drifting in the direction of the parking lot and Astrid's tent.

She slept fitfully that night and woke early. Carlita started a pot of coffee before leading Rambo outside to his favorite spot for his morning break.

Astrid's tent was gone. The empty spot filled her with a melancholy sadness. Carlita said a small prayer for the woman.

Back inside, she finished filling out the rental agreement for the new tenant, Angelica Reynolds.

Mercedes was still asleep when the moving van pulled into the alley. Carlita met them downstairs. She showed them the efficiency unit and then stood off to the side as they began unloading the furniture.

"The unit is already furnished," she told a man carrying a hot pink beaded floor lamp.

"Well, you got even more furniture now."

Next was a leopard print loveseat followed by an armoire that barely fit through the doorway. There was a bearskin rug, the snarling head of the bear clearly visible.

The man carrying the rug slowed as he passed Carlita. "Ugly, huh?"

"It's...interesting."

The men had almost finished unloading the van when a sleek, silver convertible turned the corner and pulled in behind the van.

The door opened. A woman, clad in a tangerine-tinged dress and a matching scarf tied snugly around her head, emerged. Large, dark sunglasses covered her eyes and half her face.

She stalked to the back of the moving van. "I see I'm just in time," she whispered in a raspy voice. "I trust you didn't damage any of my priceless antiques."

"Priceless antiques?" The man holding a zebra print barstool chuckled. "I wouldn't put this stuff by the curb for free."

"Why...you don't know what you're talking about." The woman pressed a hand to her chest, clearly shocked by the perceived insult. "You are a man of no class."

"Whatever." The man shrugged. "This is the last of it."

Carlita stepped closer and held out her hand. "Angelica Reynolds. I'm Carlita Garlucci, your landlord."

"Ah." Angelica turned to Carlita, smiling widely. "It's a pleasure to meet you."

"I have some paperwork upstairs, the rental agreement. I'll need your signature."

"Of course." Angelica stepped to the side to give the mover room to exit the building.

"That's everything." The man opened the cab of the van. He returned, carrying a clipboard. "You need to sign off on the delivery."

"No." Angelica shook her head. "I won't be signing anything until I've had a chance to inspect my belongings to ensure there's no damage."

"Fine." The man scribbled on the sheet, ripped off a copy and handed it to Angelica. "We won't return the deposit until you sign."

"What?" Angelica's eyes flew open and then quickly narrowed, her red lips pursed tightly together. "You'll never get another job in this town if you don't return my deposit. I'll see to it personally."

"You don't sign. You don't get your deposit back."

"Fine. Give me that." Angelica snatched the clipboard from the man's hands. She scribbled her name and handed it back. "There. You better not have damaged my belongings."

"We didn't damage anything."

354

The second mover returned to the stoop, and then the men climbed into the vehicle. The moving truck rumbled down the narrow alley before turning the corner and disappearing from sight.

Carlita pointed to Angelica's convertible. "We have one parking spot per tenant. Visitor parking is around the front of the building and on the street."

"Where is tenant parking?"

Carlita pointed to the other end of the alley. "Down there."

Angelica's eyes widened in horror. "You mean there's no covered parking?"

"No. It's not assigned parking, either. You take whatever spot is open."

"I..." Angelica's mouth snapped shut and then opened again. "Your daughter never mentioned unassigned parking to my handler."

"Handler?" Carlita asked.

"My agent."

"I'm sure she forgot."

"Well." Angelica tugged on the lapel of her dress. "I would assume then that tenants are given a discount for subpar parking."

"We don't offer a discount. Listen." Carlita was beginning to wonder what Mercedes had gotten them into with their new "tenant." "If you don't like the parking situation, there's still time to back out of the lease."

Angelica clicked her tongue. "I...just moved in."

"Then you'll have to be okay with the parking arrangement." Carlita stepped inside the building. "I'll go grab the lease agreement."

She didn't wait for the woman to reply as she climbed the steps.

The woman made a grunting noise, her angry heels clicking on the wood floor. The door to the efficiency slammed shut.

Carlita flung open the door to the apartment. "Mercedes!"

Mercedes emerged from her room. "Yeah?"

"I just met our new tenant, Angelica. What in the world did you get us into?"

The end.

If you enjoyed reading "Swiped in Savannah," would you please take a moment to leave a review? It would mean so much to me. Thank you! - Hope Callaghan

The Series Continues... Book 13 in the "Made in Savannah" Series
Coming Soon!

Books in This Series

Made in Savannah Cozy Mystery Series

Key to Savannah: Book 1
Road to Savannah: Book 2
Justice in Savannah: Book 3
Swag in Savannah: Book 4
Trouble in Savannah: Book 5
Missing in Savannah: Book 6
Setup in Savannah: Book 7
Merry Masquerade: Book 8
The Family Affair: Book 9
Pirates in Peril: Book 10
Matrimony & Mayhem: Book 11
Swiped in Savannah: Book 12
Book 13: Coming Soon!
Made in Savannah Box Set I (Books 1-3)
Made in Savannah Box Set II (Books 4-6)

Get Free Books and More

Sign up for my Free Cozy Mysteries Newsletter to get free and discounted books, giveaways & soon-to-be-released books!

hopecallaghan.com/newsletter

Meet the Author

Hope loves to connect with her readers! Connect with her today!

Never miss another book deal! Text the word Books to 33222

Visit **hopecallaghan.com/newsletter** for special offers, free books, & new releases!

Follow Hope On:

Facebook: Amazon: Pinterest:

Hope Callaghan is an American author who loves to write Christian books, especially Christian Mystery and Cozy Mystery books. She has written more than 50 mystery books (and counting) in six series.

In March 2017, Hope won a Mom's Choice Award for her book, "Key to Savannah," Book 1 in the Made in Savannah Cozy Mystery Series.

Born and raised in a small town in West Michigan, she now lives in Florida with her husband.

She is the proud mother of one daughter and a stepdaughter and stepson. When she's not doing the thing she loves best - writing books - she enjoys cooking, traveling and reading books.

Carlita's Creamy Chicken Milano Recipe

Ingredients (Sauce):

1 tbsp. butter

2 cloves garlic, minced

½ cup sun-dried tomatoes, chopped

2 cups chicken broth, divided

2 cups heavy cream

2 tbsp. cornstarch (w/ 1/8 cup cold water)

4 tbsp chopped fresh basil

Ingredients (Chicken):

1-1/2 lbs skinless, boneless chicken breasts halved

Salt and pepper to taste

2 tbsp. olive oil

12 oz. fettuccine pasta

½ cup shredded parmesan cheese

Directions:

-Melt butter in large saucepan over low heat.

-Add garlic. Sauté for half a minute.

-Add sun-dried tomatoes and 1-1/2 cup chicken broth.

-Bring to a boil. Reduce heat and simmer for ten minutes

-Add heavy cream. Bring to second boil, stirring constantly.

-Mix 2 tbsp. cornstarch with 1/8 cup cold water.

-Slowly add the cornstarch to the heavy cream mixture.

-Simmer over medium / low heat for ten minutes.

(Cooking chicken)

-Season both sides of chicken with salt and pepper.

-Add olive oil to large skillet. Cook chicken in large skillet over medium heat.

-Cook chicken, turning occasionally for 12 minutes or until internal temperature is 165 degrees F. or greater.

-Remove from skillet and set aside to cool.

-Deglaze skillet w/chicken. (Mix with remaining broth to capture the flavors of the meat.)

-Add chicken broth to creamy mixture in saucepan.

-Stir in basil. Set aside until fettuccine finishes cooking.

-Cook fettuccine 10-12 minutes or until al dente.

-After cooking, drain pasta.

-Add creamy mixture and cooked chicken.

-Season with salt and pepper to taste.

-Plate and serve with topping of parmesan cheese.